Maur

NO FIXED ADDRESS

cover art by
Ginette Beaulieu

Scholastic Canada
Toronto, New York, London, Sydney, Auckland

Scholastic Canada Ltd.
123 Newkirk Road, Richmond Hill, Ontario, Canada L4C 3G5

Scholastic Inc.
555 Broadway, New York, NY 10012, USA

Scholastic Australia Pty Limited
PO Box 579, Gosford, NSW 2250, Australia

Scholastic New Zealand Limited
Private Bag 94407, Greenmount, Auckland, New Zealand

Scholastic Publications Ltd.
Villiers House, Clarendon Avenue, Leamington Spa, Warwickshire
CV32 5PR, UK

Canadian Cataloguing in Publication Data
Bayless, Maureen, 1959-
 No fixed address

ISBN 0-590-12378-5

I. Title.

PS8553.A85855N6 1997   jC813'.54   C97-930202-1
PZ7.B39No 1997

5 4 3 2 1   Printed in Canada   7 8 9/9

For Sam, Jacob, David and Noah.
And for Danna Megan, wherever you are.

The author would like to thank: John and Vi Colclough for childcare and pumpkin pie; Alan Bayless, for the ever-replenished supply of chocolate; Judy and Isaac Thau, for the gift of their Mac; Charlotte Gordon for her tireless efforts as agent; and Laura Peetoom, for her kind words and guiding editorial hand.

Chapter One

The 9-1-1 operator wanted to keep her on the phone, but Sabie didn't want to be there when the ambulance came. If she was, Social Services would get her for sure. And Monika always said that was the one thing you didn't want to let happen.

"Just come," she pleaded, and hung up.

The phone booth she was in stood just outside the banged-up door of the Kingscrest. Feeling like she might be sick, Sabie closed her eyes, leaning against the glass. The stale, cigarettey smell of the booth and the muffled sound of the Commercial Drive traffic made her feel almost as if she were at home again, in her room in the Kingscrest which looked out at this very spot.

"Move your butt, kid," someone said, smacking the door.

Without lifting her eyes, Sabie slipped out of the booth and cut across the street to the Hillside

Drug Mart. Tires squealed and someone swore at her, but she felt as barely connected to herself as her shadow and didn't look up.

By the time she got to the Drug Mart window, a fire truck was pulling up. Why had they sent a fire truck? she wondered. There was no fire, though she'd always worried about one, the way some of the drunks smoked in bed. She'd been sure the whole peeling, bug-infested building would burn down one day. Maybe it still would.

"They'd never send a truck here," Monika used to warn their neighbours. "If you don't pay taxes, you're not worth a sow bug's breath in this town. And that's a fact."

"A fire, Dad!" A little boy dragged his dad from the cash line and out onto the pavement to gawk.

Already a crowd was gathering. Sabie had to move around it to watch an ambulance nose in behind the fire truck. After what seemed a long, long time, two men came through the door of the Kingscrest with a stretcher.

"Omygawd, it's a *body!*" squealed a teenager, burying her face in her boyfriend's shoulder. Sabie started at the squeal, and bumped against the lottery counter.

"They're not hurrying with *that* one," observed the boyfriend. "Probably another knifing. Drugs or something. Happens around here all the time."

Even though the stretcher was covered, Sabie could tell which end was the head and which end was the feet. But if she hadn't already known, she wouldn't have been able to tell who was strapped under the blanket. The shape was unfamiliar, unnatural. Nobody lies flat out like that in real life, she thought. So neat and tidy and unprotected.

The attendants folded the wheels up under the stretcher and slid it into the ambulance. A policewoman, sipping from a paper coffee cup, said something to the men.

Then for awhile nothing happened and the crowd began to drift away. The boy and his father, the two teenagers, even the cup of coffee were long gone before the ambulance pulled away from the curb. The driver didn't bother to put the siren on. That bothered Sabie a lot. It didn't seem right that a life should end so insignificantly, drawing no more notice than a passing taxi.

She could hear the busker outside the liquor store crooning "Bird on a Wire" but he sounded more like a Rottweiler than Leonard Cohen. Monika would raise her eyebrows if she heard how he was murdering that song, Sabie decided, thinking of all the times the two of them had sat on the stone step of the Kingscrest, tapping their toes to other buskers. And the times they themselves had busked, drawing the smiles and change of passersby, below the Skytrain. Then she shivered.

She focussed on reclaiming her corduroy backpack from the lottery counter where she had dropped it, slipping her arms through the straps and stepping out of the drugstore. Up the street, the ambulance turned onto Twelfth and disappeared.

"Bye, Mom," she whispered.

Sabie Pincher, age thirteen, was on her own.

Chapter Two

Sabie trudged along the street, head down against the stinging reach of the sun, and was pierced by the brilliant shades of red, blue and green on the gum wrappers and chip bags that had wedged into corners and crevices. Vaguely, she wondered at that — hadn't litter always before seemed grey? She hugged Monika's quilted guitar case and narrowed her eyes until the shimmering sidewalk was as slight as a fingernail paring.

They'd known for a long time that Monika was going to die, that she had cancer. Cancer was the reason Monika had taken Sabie into hiding after Sabie's father, Colin, had gone to Calgary to marry Other Woman. Sabie had been just a kindergarten-aged kid then, trying to figure out why she had a new name ("You're Sabie Struthers now, not Sabie Pincher," Monika had said) and no place in particular to live.

Monika had tried to explain, but her explanation had only added to Sabie's confusion and fright. Monika, vague and distracted as she had been since Colin had moved away from Nelson, had pulled Sabie toward her and stroked her hair. "I'm sick, but I don't want Colin to find out," she'd said, with an urgency in her voice that Sabie hadn't understood. "He doesn't want you, really doesn't want you, and if I go to the hospital he'll give you to Social Services. Then you'll be stuck with some foster family. Who knows how they'll treat you? At the very least, they'll try to make you just like everybody else. And you're special, a free spirit, like me."

That had begun their life in hiding, and really, their preparation for this day. They had moved to Vancouver, where they'd kept on moving, making sure nobody got to know them too well. Monika had found live-in baby-sitting jobs as often as she could, or they had made do in empty, soon-to-be-torn-down houses. They stayed out of shelters and, mostly, away from the street kids who hung around the downtown strip: social worker bait, Monika called them.

Sabie had been home–schooled, a special program designed by her mother to prepare Sabie to live on her own, away from the clutches of the social workers. Monika told Sabie she wanted her to have an authority-questioning life, completely unlike the nine-to-five suburban life Colin had chosen after leaving Monika and their band, Blue Karma.

On dry days, Sabie and Monika fished newspapers out of trash cans and read them in the sun, Monika always asking Sabie what she thought about this and that: adoption, aboriginal land claims, immigration. Rainy days, they went down under the bridge and watched boats being put together, or delivered flyers for pay. Regularly, they took Monika's guitar and Sabie's violin down to Kits Beach and busked, which meant leaving Monika's hand-stitched guitar case open so that people could drop money into it.

"Busking's something that you'll be able to do even after," Monika had told Sabie, meaning after she died and Sabie was on her own.

From the age of six, Sabie had been preparing for this moment, preparing to fend for herself. Though she had believed her mother's death was forever in the future, she'd always known it was coming; she could taste it in their time together, just the way you could taste salt in the Fraser where it neared the sea. Whenever Sabie grew angry over having to leave yet another home, she had only to take one look at Monika's tired, patient face to remember that Monika had chosen Sabie over medical treatment and a chance at life.

Monika had taught her daughter that in other times children had worked in factories, farmed, mined, even married. There was no reason why Sabie couldn't learn to look after herself. She expected Sabie to think independently, though not selfishly, and taught her to work and forage. Sabie knew how to make a home anywhere: in a hedge, a hollow beach log, an empty metal drum, a school playground, a burned-out garage.

And now, Sabie knew where she was heading:

to the backyard jumble of car wrecks that Monika had picked to be their next shelter — they had run out of rent money. The sidewalk Sabie followed was thick with shoppers and tourists, some of them smelling of sunscreen. They flowed by her like water around a stone, not seeing her. Once a couple, holding hands, raised their arms like a bridge for her to pass under.

Sabie walked with a cold numb feeling; it was as if a boulder had settled inside her and was choking off the blood flow to her legs. An alley cat, lean and fast, darted between the wheels of a recycling truck and skidded nimbly around a dumpster. "Cats always land on their feet," Sabie remembered Monika saying, "And you will too, my little alley urchin." Would she?

She turned the corner onto a street lined with boxy brick walk-ups. Heavy-headed and syrupy, her feet gumming to the sunburnt asphalt, Sabie reached inside her numb self for a bit of Monika to help her. Something to frame things, make her understand what Monika expected of her now.

A memory came to her.

A home-schooling day one November. Sabie was about eleven. They were standing on the beach at Jericho, alone. The tide was out and the mud flats shone like ice.

"What's the biggest question on your mind today?" Monika asked. She was wearing faded jeans and a cable sweater, and the wind and her smile made her grey eyes shine.

"Umm," stalled Sabie, dragging her toe in the

sand to make a heart. She was used to this question. Monika always asked it, but one of the rules was that Sabie couldn't bring a question with her to the beach. It had to be one from the moment. One straight from the heart.

"You're thinking too hard," said Monika. She bumped Sabie with her hip. Sabie had to jump aside; the sand heart zagged out of shape. Then Monika grasped Sabie's hands in her own.

"Ask me," she instructed, and began spinning in a circle. Almost immediately, Sabie was lifted off her feet.

"What?" cried Sabie, beginning to giggle and feeling angry at Monika for making her giggle when she was trying to think.

"Ask me your important questions!" called Monika, spinning in a wider circle, taking them across the mud of Jericho. Sabie was sometimes in the air, skimming the ground like a gull, sometimes catching the wet, silty sand with her toes and almost falling into it. But Monika never stopped turning, even when she was dragging Sabie. "Ask me the questions you'll want to ask when I'm gone!"

Sabie grunted, running to keep up. What questions? Which questions? But she tried.

"What's going to happen to me — after?"

Monika's face bobbed before her, smudged against the sullen sky. "Not that kind of stuff!" Monika exclaimed, puffing. "Not the stuff about where you'll live. That's not important. Ask me the ones you would ask God if you believed in God!"

Monika spun faster.

Sabie's arms twisted. She fell on her hip in the wet, silty sand. "What are you doing?" she cried, half laughing, half annoyed.

"Dance!" urged Monika, lifting her head to the sky. "Go with me!"

Sabie struggled to run with Monika and in a moment she was airborne again, Monika spinning round and round and round.

"Ask!" Without warning, Monika changed the direction of her spin. Sabie bellyflopped into the sand.

"Whoops!" exclaimed Monika, pausing just long enough for Sabie to brush the grit from her stomach and knees. "Well, never mind. Think harder. What's on your mind?"

Sabie grabbed Monika's hands again and ran as fast as she could around her mother as Monika turned. Sabie's thoughts were jumbled and pounding. The edge of her foot clipped a log and questions burst from her with the pain: "Why do I have to have a sick mother? Why do I have to be different from other kids? And who's going to be my friend or even care about me when you're gone? It's not fair!"

Her questions were snatched away by the wind. Monika didn't say anything, didn't say that Sabie's questions were good or dumb. Her eyes were closed, her head still thrown back, her feet still hurrying, and Sabie saw for the first time that there were tears on Monika's cheeks.

"Dance," Monika said, softly.

Sabie shut her eyes, too. She threw back her head like Monika and stopped thinking.

With her eyes shut, Sabie could feel through Monika's hands the direction she was going. It was easier to follow her then. She could hear Monika's breathing, three breaths to each break of a wave. Monika's hands pulled, pulled, and now Sabie no longer flew or was dragged, but wheeled with her. They were dancing! Kicking the sand with their feet, spinning to the music of the waves, the pull of each other's arms keeping them both from collapsing backward into the sand.

Finally, Monika dropped to the ground, panting, laughing. Sabie settled beside her, nestling into Monika's warmth to ward off the wet chill of the sand. "You're kinda wacko, Mom, you know," she said.

"Mm-hmm," Monika agreed. "But what do you get from this?"

"Hunh?" Sabie, on her back, shaded her eyes to keep out the whirling sky. She had almost forgotten what had started their exhilarating run.

A dog charged along the sand, chasing a stick that someone had thrown into the water. Plunging into the breakers, he disappeared for a moment, then emerged from the spray with a stick in his jaws.

Monika raised her head. "When you one day wonder what your life is all about, or what to do about some big thing, or how to find a way to make something good out of something not so good, how are you going to find your answer?"

Sabie thought about the way that they had spun on the beach. How she hadn't been able to keep up with Monika until she'd stopped trying. Until she'd closed her eyes and let herself be carried along.

"Life's about going along with things?" she guessed.

Monika laughed. "Like hanging with a bad crowd?" She threw a few grains of sand at Sabie. "No, not exactly. It's about dancing with whatever gets thrown your way, about looking for your own rhythm, your own answers. Life's a kind of dance step, whirling you and throwing you. It rushes at you and whomps you in the gut . . . " She jabbed Sabie in the ribs and Sabie giggled. "You get tired, you get winded, but you keep going. You make something amazing out of it. It's better than the way some people live, like Colin, letting other people pave their way for them. And you *have* to dance, or else . . . "

"Or else you fall," Sabie summed up.

Monika slipped her hand into Sabie's. "I'm so sorry that I won't be with you, pet. But — when we were dancing, didn't you feel the wind on your face? The sand under your feet?"

"Stones on my knees — "

"Whatever," said Monika, wiping an eye with the back of a sandy arm. "That'll be your hug. That'll be your friend, your family. Ups and downs, struggle and stillness, finding and losing, meaning and no meaning, it's all in life, your dancing partner. So hold on tight — and dance!"

Now, trudging along Twelfth Avenue, making her way through the first hours of life without Monika, her mother, her teacher, her family, Sabie knew that she was going to begin the dance of life.

And tried to believe that she could do it without Monika to pull her along.

Chapter Three

Stopping only once, to rest from the sun inside the tent-like branches of the ancient evergreens on the Cambie Street boulevard, Sabie made her way to a house on Carr Avenue. She didn't have to think about that; her feet simply carried her there. She and Monika had walked that way often, of late.

"The Ritz of urban campsites!" Monika had pronounced just two weeks ago, when they'd made their find. They'd been cutting through an alley on their way to the public washroom at Children's Hospital when Monika suddenly vaulted over a rusted-out garbage can to inspect. Crammed willy-nilly into the backyard of a dilapidated old house were five apparently abandoned cars, grass growing like grain around and through them. Even if somebody had wanted to drive them away, they'd have had to cut down the blueberry bushes and lilac saplings that had sprung up against the alley.

"Handy. Very, very handy," Monika said glee-fully, taking a sip from the crumbling black hose that was coiled against the flaking shingle wall.

Then, bunching back the unruly curls that had dangled into the hose water, she had directed Sabie to score the site.

Sabie knew what Monika meant. She was sup-posed to list the things about this yard that would make it a good urban campsite, and grade them. She did this all the time. It was part of her survival training.

"No neighbours on that side," Sabie said, after assessing things. "That house is really new and it looks like the owners haven't moved in yet. Ten points. There's a fairly high fence on that side and a really high one on this side. Ten. There are blue-berry bushes and raspberry canes here and there are strawberry plants up against the house. The people on the other side of the alley have a vegetable garden. So there's stuff to eat. A little, anyway. Eight."

"But what can you tell about whoever lives here?" Monika asked.

Sabie shrugged. "They don't come into the backyard much?" she guessed. Weeds had nearly swallowed an old electric mower that had been left in the middle of the yard, possibly years ago.

"Look at those brocade curtains in the windows, all faded, and the knick-knacks. I don't think a bunch of university students would go for that. Probably an old lady, half-blind and half-crippled," declared Monika. "Not the kind to cause trouble.

That's ten points! Nearly forty points, and anything over thirty-two is fabulous. Yep, this place will make a great fall-back."

Now, as Sabie paused at the edge of the yard, fingering the rough, lichen-covered branch of a lilac, vaguely lulled by the summer smells of alley dust and warm grass, she felt as though she were viewing it all through a time-defying bubble: the fenced rectangle of weeds before her held her future and as long as she paused here, one foot in the alley, she could postpone time. Her heart no longer needed to beat, and all was silent. Then a pickup turned into the alley, grinding gravel under its wheels, and like a startled squirrel she leapt out of the bubble and behind a power pole. This was it, then. She was going on.

"You'll be just like a modern day Robinson Crusoe when I'm gone," Monika had promised Sabie many times. "Making your own way in the urban forest, carving a life for yourself with your bare hands and wit." Robinson Crusoe, it occured to Sabie now, had landed on soft, tree-rimmed sand, not on a hard patch of creosote-soaked dirt below the windows of a stranger. The island before her was just somebody's backyard. And she was just a kid.

Sabie crept into the yard, pushing away the thick-stemmed, bush-high weeds with her palms. When she reached the hose, she took a drink, as Monika had. The water was warm, rubbery, as Monika must have found it. Sabie stood just where Monika had stood and surveyed her situation with Monika's eyes.

Monika had named all five of the junked cars: Mustang Mansion, Valiant Villa, Bungalow BelAir, Chateau Chrysler, and the leaky starter special, Pinto Place. Chateau Chrysler, a hardtop with the least mould on its wide bench seats, was Sabie's choice. It had two working windows.

Moving efficiently and quietly to avoid detection, she pushed her backpack and Monika's guitar in and smoothly followed, pulling the door shut behind her. It slammed with a *whoomp*, and she lay pressed against the plastic upholstery in case anybody had heard, one knee on the floor, the seat soon reflecting heat back at her with real-person warmth.

"Mom," she said, involuntarily.

She lay still for a long, long time.

The hot midday sun cut in through the greasy glass, raising a mildewy, nauseating hot-vinyl-and-old-cigarette smell. Sabie pulled Monika's quilted guitar case close and pressed her nose against it. Its colours swam before her eyes, the pieced-together-from-old-clothes image of a mother and child running into the smooth satin mountains and sky.

Sabie had a strong sense of being in a foreign land, as if she had followed a familiar map but arrived at the wrong destination. Bluebottles buzzed, recalling the police car's whining engine and the murmuring of the crowd at the Kingscrest.

She slept.

When she woke, it was late afternoon. As Robinson Crusoe had, she took stock of her possessions, emptying the backpack onto the rubber floor mat.

First, of course, was her violin. She'd played fiddle since before she could remember, and when she set up on a sidewalk, even if Monika wasn't backing her up on guitar, she could draw crowds — and money. Fiddling was like a language to Sabie. Sometimes, she felt it was her first language.

There wasn't much else in her pack. A T-shirt, a sunhat, rosin for the violin bow, a pair of dirty socks that she had taken off and forgotten the last time she was at Kits Beach. Half of a novel she'd found in the beach washroom, *The Not Impossible Summer*. Monika had torn it in two so they could read it at the same time. Wedged into the pouch, she found a forgotten photo of Monika standing before a Volkswagen van. It was really half a photo, Colin's half having been torn off. There was nothing left of him but one shoe, black with black laces, planted next to Monika's sandalled toes. Sabie, on her back in the Chrysler, gazed at the frayed-edged shoe for several long minutes. That short, wide foot was all that remained of her father, the bass player who had lived with Monika on and off before he'd finally gone off to Calgary with someone else.

Then Sabie slipped the photo back into the pouch. Thinking of her father was less useful than counting socks. Colin had never wanted to be a father, Monika had told her many times. Anyway, Robinson Crusoe didn't go knocking on virtual strangers' doors for help.

Over the next week, Sabie made of Chateau Chrysler a home of sorts. She found an old cloth under the rotted back porch. It was hard with dirt or age, but, moistened with a little hose water, it made a good scouring rag. Working at night by window-light, Sabie dipped her rag into the sand that edged the alley and scrubbed the Chrysler clean of mildew. She couldn't get rid of the smell, but she battled it with lilacs, while they lasted, and then crushed mint.

She began to notice the rhythms of the woman who lived in the shake house. Each morning, the woman came down the front steps and trimmed the front lawn with kitchen scissors, leaving the dande-lion heads where they fell. Sabie was careful then to keep to the back, out of sight, but she could see that the woman was elderly and frail. She could stand only with support and the front stairs had no railing, so she had to crawl. At twilight the light in the brocade-curtained room — probably a dining room — was turned on and left on all night. Its light would shine softly over the backyard like a neon sign over a car lot, and Sabie would sleep, some-times dreaming that Monika was at the wheel of the Chrysler and that they were speeding toward a fat, mottled moon.

After a few days of stealing cheese from the Dairyland truck and chives and rhubarb from the neighbour's garden, Sabie returned to busking. This was hard. Her fiddle sounded hollow without Monika, not only because Monika had usually ac-companied her but because Monika had always been there, smiling, listening. Now, each note fell into silence, unmet, and Sabie's fingers tangled self-consciously over the strings. Even "Turkey in the Straw" came out jumbled and wistful and the bow slipped and whistled "Monika!"

Sabie tried different locations and soon learned to play in the doorway of the Main Street McDonald's, against the cement block wall of the Plaza Fruit Market, so that the fiddle's sound was filled out and rounded by an echo. Her second day there the McDonald's manager, a brown-skinned lady who smelled of tangerines, gave her a wrapped Filet-o-Fish and a shake and paid her five dollars to play "Happy Birthday" to a crowd of six-year-olds. On another afternoon a teenager came out of Main Aquarium and handed her a bag of guppies. Sabie set them on her fiddle towel amidst the coins and bills until a boy admired them and took them home in the basket of his wheelchair.

Two weeks after Monika's death Sabie returned to the Kingscrest and stood just where she had when the ambulance had come. There was somebody new in their old room. Did the new tenant with the radio that now propped open their window have all their things, Monika's meditation journal and their clothes? Sabie wondered. Did their room still smell the way that Monika always made a room smell, of burning sage and incense? Sabie, unable to launder her things because she did not have anything else to wear, smelled of Chateau Chrysler. She longed to smell that Monika smell just one more time.

People streamed along the littered sidewalk, crowding onto buses, stepping over the legs of the drunk who had fallen asleep under a newspaper, sipping mugs of Starbucks coffee or licking peaks of soft ice cream. Nobody seemed to notice that the centre of Sabie's world had disappeared on this very spot. Nobody paused to comment on the girl who stood so long, staring across the street at a bit of flapping curtain.

"You've got to dance with life," Monika had said. "You've got to use every day until it's a juiced-out orange."

A Dickie Dee ice cream truck, blaring some tinkly tune, pulled up against a fire hydrant in front of Sabie, and the driver, cursing, hopped out to examine his bumper.

"Did you see that guy whack me?" he cried to no one in particular, and Sabie, turning away with a mumble, realized she hadn't heard her own voice in four days.

Chapter Four

Sabie grew so used to living in Chateau Chrysler that she forgot to worry about being discovered. Nobody ever visited, no flashlights ever probed her hiding place. Then one morning she awoke to the sound of voices.

" . . . old bag!" a girl exclaimed. "What's she think she's doing, keeping all this stuff down there? She'll never use any of it. Probably doesn't know what she has."

Footsteps scraped by the car, and Sabie pressed herself into the seat. The acrid smell of mould stung her throat. She looked at Monika's watch. It wasn't even five A.M.

The old lady's being robbed, she thought.

Thud. Something heavy was put down somewhere.

"Not like that," a guy said, impatiently. "Leave room for this." The thing, whatever it was, was moved.

Should I stop them? Sabie wondered. Jump out

at them like I live here or something?

Just then, the back door squeaked.

"Get out of here!" the old woman cried. "I called the police! Go away!"

"Up yours, Estelle," retorted the guy, not sounding at all bothered. Footsteps went by Sabie to the house again.

"Got the box, Mark?"

Mark grunted, obviously a *yes*. "Take another look, see what else there is," he said.

"Didn't you hear me?" the old lady yelled. "I said I called the police. The police are coming!"

"Yeah? Well, we have every right to this stuff, and you know it!" Mark hollered back.

Sabie rolled onto the floor of the car, considering her situation. If she got out of the car now, she'd be seen for sure. She could make a run for it, but Mark and the girl would probably pack Monika's guitar in with the other stuff. They had a car or van; she could hear its engine running. On the other hand, if she waited here, the police would come and that would be worse.

"Stop it! How can you do this? Stop it!" quavered the old woman — Estelle — banging something, probably her cane, against the wall.

The two thieves paused by Chateau Chrysler. "Maybe we should leave, Mark. She might have a stroke or something." The girl spoke in an anxious whisper.

"Cut the crap, Sheryl," replied Mark, not bothering to keep his voice down. "It's now or never. You know that."

"Oh my, oh my," Estelle moaned, over and over. Sabie heard a car door bang. She peeped over the rim of the door to see Mark getting into a maroon station wagon. He was just a young guy, tall and thin with straight brown hair. He looked barely old enough to drive. Staring through the window on the passenger's side was Sheryl, with narrow shoulders and brown hair very like Mark's.

The car peeled away, sending gravel flying up the alley.

"Oh my, oh God . . . "

Sabie looked up at the groaning woman, who was gripping the railing of the rotting porch, bending over it as if she'd taken a blow to the stomach. Or maybe, Sabie reflected, her back was always bent that way, from hunching over her cane.

As if the slight breeze that flicked the leaves of the lilacs had overturned her, the old woman twisted backwards and settled to the ground like a dropped tissue.

No police were in sight. Sabie unlatched the car door and slipped out.

"Hello?" she called, softly. The figure above her did not move.

The bottom three stairs of the back porch were missing, the wood rotted right through. Sabie reached for the next one, to pull herself up, but it came away in her hands.

"Great," she muttered. "Just great."

Didn't the neighbours around here have ears? Why weren't they out here, beating off those robbers? So what if it was the crack of dawn!

It came to her that Mark and Sheryl could not have carried stuff down these stairs, that they must have been using the basement door that adjoined the shed. Checking, she found the door ajar.

She entered, blinking in the dimness. Right away, she banged her knee. When her eyes adjusted to the light she saw to her amazement that the basement was filled floor to ceiling with . . . things. All kinds of things. Rusty tricycles and seatless bicycles. Lamps, boxes, torn chairs perched one atop another. Dolls, bears, games in broken boxes. Plastic bottles of cola, a whole mountain of paper-wrapped matzo cracker boxes.

She felt like she had walked into a mammoth garage sale.

One hand before her to steady any tippy towers, she followed the narrow clearing to the stairs and went up them. The stairs themselves were lined with shoes, old telephones, and jars of peanut butter. Unopened peanut butter. More than an old woman could ever eat.

There was no doubt about it, the lady was crazy. Crazy as a poisoned bedbug, Monika would have said. But, crazy or not, she couldn't be left out back like that, maybe to die.

At the top of the stairs was a door which opened into a narrow hallway. There the musty basement smell gave way to an overpowering stench. Sabie's stomach lurched violently, and she was almost sick. What *was* that?

She looked into the kitchen. It too was stacked high with stuff, and it took her a moment to make sure that there was no door leading outside. Next to the kitchen was a smaller room, painted yellow.

"Ugh!" Sabie drew back in horror. In the corner was the source of the smell — a dead dog. There were flies everywhere.

"Oh my, oh my," Sabie heard Estelle moaning, weakly. Through a screen door that opened into the room, Sabie could see the old woman stirring, pushing up onto her hands and knees.

"Estelle?" Sabie called, going outside to her. She didn't look at the dog as she passed.

Blood trickled down Estelle's face, wending its way through the landscape of wrinkles to her chin. Some had dribbled onto Estelle's nightgown. The nightgown, Sabie noticed, had been pulled on over a blue dress.

"You're bleeding," Sabie observed with concern, pulling Estelle's arm to help her up.

Estelle screamed. "Not that arm! That's my bad arm. Oh, you're as bad as that devil, you are!"

So Sabie just stood, helping out as best she could while Estelle pulled herself up, using both Sabie and the railing as handholds.

"Maybe you should go inside and sit down," Sabie suggested anxiously, wondering how fragile old ladies were.

"Don't be *meshuggah!*" gasped Estelle. "You think I want blood all over the house?"

"But — "

"Can't you get a cloth? A wet one?"

"Unh . . . " Sabie hurried back into the house and into the kitchen. She found a dirty tea towel sitting on the stove top and held it under the tap. No water came out. Neither hot nor cold.

The injured woman, probably guessing what had happened, called in to her. "Not that sink! Oh, don't you know anything? That sink hasn't worked in years! Use the one in the utility room."

Which room was the utility room? Sabie had no idea. Madly, she ran about the house, bumping into things wherever she went. The main floor, a simple neighbouring of small living room, hall, bathroom and bedroom, was hardly less cluttered and gloomy than the basement. All the overstuffed furniture, the curtains and the rugs had faded to the same pale, pinky brown. The taps in the bathroom sink did not work either. Nor did the bathtub.

Sabie found, at last, that the utility room was the dog room. An old laundry tub in it had taps that let off a rusty stream of water. She hurried back outside.

"Here," Sabie said, relieved to have it over with.

"What took you so long?" grumbled Estelle, snatching the towel. Sabie, watching, saw that the woman couldn't stand and wipe her face at the same time, but kept letting go of the cloth to grab the railing. Finally, Sabie did it for her, pressing the cut until the bleeding stopped.

"It doesn't look as bad as I thought," she said. What did look bad was Estelle's face: she didn't have any teeth.

Once reunited with her cane, Estelle made her shuffling way down the hall to the sofa, into which she sank with a moan. "I hate that devil!" she said, with bitter passion. "Oh, if I could kill her, I would."

"Sheryl?" Sabie guessed.

Estelle blinked at her. "No, not Sheryl, you fool. Her mother, the devil. The devil! Those kids are bad, but they've just got their mother's poison — "

"Well," said Sabie soothingly, having no clue what Estelle was talking about, "the police will be here soon, I guess."

"The police!" Estelle shouted. She had, Sabie noticed, rather a habit of shouting. "I didn't call the police! That's just what she wants, isn't it?"

"What?"

"The police! She wants the police. They'd put me in the Louis Brier Home, that's what they'd do. And then she'd have everything."

Sabie decided to change the subject. "Did you know there's a dead dog in your utility room?" she asked. Maybe Estelle's nose wasn't working.

"Of course there's a dead dog in the utility room," retorted Estelle huffily. "Do you think I could get it down the back stairs? At my age?"

Wondering what to make of that, Sabie sat in silence. Should she help this old lady get changed? She was spotted with blood. And the layers of dirt on the thick pink socks had been there a long, long time. Or maybe she should call an ambulance. It could be that the bump on her head was the reason Estelle wasn't making any sense.

"*You* could," Estelle said. Holding the cloth against her head, and sagged back in her chair, she was peering intently at her visitor.

"Could what?" asked Sabie, thinking that perhaps it was time to slip out the door and get back to real life.

"Bury the dog!" Estelle replied. "What else? You think I want it lying around my utility room? It was bad enough that I had to trip over it when it was alive, poor blind untrained old thing. Why should I break my neck over it now that it's dead?"

Sabie stood up. "I don't think so," she said weakly. She didn't think she could even sit around any longer in the foul air of the living room, visiting, let alone get any closer to that — thing.

"What do you mean, you don't think so?" barked Estelle. "Don't give me that 'I don't think so' stuff. You've been living in my backyard for days. Don't think I didn't see you! Now, you get out there and bury old Henry!"

Chapter Five

"Are the police after you?" Estelle asked, squinting at Sabie. While Sabie had been out back, burying Henry, Estelle had put her teeth in and taken her nightgown off.

"No," answered Sabie, rubbing her hands on her shorts. She'd scrubbed in the utility room, but could still smell Henry on herself. It was sickening.

"Oh," said Estelle.

Sabie thought Estelle sounded disappointed.

"Could I wash my clothes in your sink?" she asked. The last thing she wanted to do was busk in the hot sun smelling of Henry. Maybe Estelle had a blanket or robe to lend her while the clothes dried.

"You are much smaller than Ginny," Estelle said.

"Right," replied Sabie, not sure what to make of that. She moved toward the utility room. "I'll just wash up and be out of here, okay?" This old lady was bats.

She had left the door open in the utility room, and thrown Henry's blankets over the porch. It still smelled bad, but with the breeze blowing through, it was tolerable. Sabie stripped off her clothes, dropped them into the deep concrete basin, and turned on the water. When the basin was half full of steaming, soapy water it looked so inviting that she hopped in too. No sense passing up a good bath.

She sank into the water, knees up against her chin, the rough concrete cool against her back. It had been a long time since she'd soaked like this. At the Kingscrest, she and Monika had used the shower down the hall. They had stood guard for each other while they were dressing, so that men wouldn't wander in to use the toilet.

She wondered whether the police had found out Monika's real name yet. She'd given a fake name to the Kingscrest so that Colin couldn't track them down, if he was looking. Which Sabie doubted. Maybe Monika would be "Serena Starr" forever and ever; strangers would walk past her grave and wonder who Serena Starr had been and if her life had been as pretty as her name. Whereas Monika Pincher would officially never die.

Sabie suddenly grew aware of a sliding, grunting noise in the hallway. She opened her eyes. It sounded like Henry was dragging himself back from the dead.

It wasn't Henry, of course. It was Estelle. She came into the utility room on her hands and knees, the shape of her bony shoulders poking through her sweater. She was dragging a green garbage bag behind her.

Sabie peered over the edge of the laundry tub. This lady was getting weirder and weirder. Sabie suddenly realized she didn't have a towel. Great, just great.

"Morty kept all this," Estelle said, panting a little because she was out of breath. "I used to tell him to give it to the Sally Ann, but he never did. Oh, I yelled at him for that."

"Your husband?" Sabie guessed.

"No, no!" Estelle barked, as if Sabie had suggested Morty was an axe-murderer. "Not my husband, who was such a bargain I could spit. Oh, he ruined my life, my husband did." She plucked at the plastic bag, dragging it nearer.

Morty wasn't the husband, then. But who was he? Actually, Sabie didn't really care who Morty was. The water was getting cold. She felt trapped, suspended in the laundry tub above Estelle's head. She wondered whether the best thing to do would be to fish her clothes out from under her legs, leap out of the tub and make a run for it.

"Morty was my son, God rest him. I loved him. But he was a *chazer*. You know what a *chazer* is?" Estelle looked up at Sabie expectantly, not seeming to notice that Sabie was in her sink. They might have been having a chat over cookies.

Sabie shook her head. "Do you have a towel?"

Estelle ignored this. "A pig. A *chazer* is a pig. A *chazer* leaves his old mother all day long with a dog that messes on the carpet. A *chazer* knows the dog has bladder problems and the mother could break her ankle just getting caught in the chain when she opens the door for him, but the *chazer* only thinks about how fun it would be to go on a scenic ferry ride."

Her eyes sparked. "See, I know some Yiddish still, from my mother. We lived too far from Saskatoon to get good Jewish schooling, but my mother made sure we all could speak Yiddish. Of course, Ginny was the smartest, but I learned too."

Estelle brushed away a fat green fly. "Henry was sick, did I tell you? I told Morty he should be put down, but Morty loved him too much. He didn't walk him, but he loved him. That dog gave him more affection than his own children." She was silent a moment, scraping dirt off the linoleum with her nail. "I'm glad the dog's dead. He was lonely. And the body lying there like that, it made me think of Morty."

Sabie did not want to think about dead bodies. The whole thing about what happens after death had been on her mind a lot lately. Shuddering, she found her shirt and wrung it out. Draping it over the narrow lip of the basin, she reached in and fished out her shorts. Stained as they were with tree sap and car grease, it would take more than warm water to get them clean.

"Perfect!" Estelle said, gleefully tugging something blue and white from the bag. "Ginny bought this on her last trip to Israel, after the '67 war. Lovely she looked in it, too."

"Great," Sabie said, trying to sound enthusiastic. She considered the possibilities of escape.

"Put it on."

"Huh?"

"Put it on! Why do you think I dragged it all the way here, in my condition? You need something to wear. Here is a dress. Put it on."

Swallowing hard, Sabie lowered her pruney body over the edge of the sink. The linoleum floor felt sticky under her feet. She wished she had stepped into her sandals.

"You're all bones," Estelle said, examining her critically. "Doesn't your mother feed you?"

Sabie took the dress from Estelle and lowered it over her own head. Even Estelle laughed when it was on. Made of heavy cotton with cut-glass diamonds around the scooped neckline, it had obviously been intended for a large woman. The gathered bust sagged, the armhole openings hung so low all of Sabie's ribs showed through and, worst of all, the neckline was so deep that, as far as modesty was concerned, she might just as well have worn nothing.

"Ginny was a full-figured woman," Estelle said, smiling up from her position on the floor. "But, don't worry. You'll grow. You'll grow."

Not soon enough, Sabie thought.

In the end she wore a flouncy synthetic blouse under the dress. Estelle's bag, it turned out, was filled with Ginny's clothes, mostly short-skirted dresses that were ankle length when held against Sabie. Morty had brought them home after Ginny's funeral more than a decade ago, and the bag, Estelle said, had been sitting in the front closet since then.

"He liked to keep things, Morty did. And what for, I ask. A lot of good it can do him now." Estelle crawled down the hall, making her painful way between piles of soda cans, phone books and shoes. The old patterned carpet was rubbed thin of colour down the middle. "But maybe he was right about Ginny's clothes. You can't buy quality like that these days, not for any price."

Sabie watched Estelle go down the hall, then gathered up her wet clothes and laid them out on the back porch to dry. In the sun, it wouldn't take more than an hour or two before she could wear them, she figured. Until then, she'd just have to hide out here in Ginny's clothes. She felt strange in the musty-smelling dress, as if she were wearing a costume for a play but didn't have her lines yet. The blouse felt scratchy.

"Hello, there!" Sabie heard someone calling from across the alley. Standing in the vegetable patch that Sabie had so recently raided was a sinewy, grey-haired woman.

"You must be Sheryl," the woman said, waving a trowel at her.

Sabie drew closer to the porch post.

"About time you started coming to see your grandmother," the woman called cheerily. "I thought after Morty died you might start coming round. I know that you and your father weren't close after the divorce, so . . . " She looked stricken. "Oh my," she exclaimed. "I always say too much. Well, the important thing is, you're here now and that will do Estelle a world of good, I'm sure. She's been looking so peaky since Morty passed on, you know. Poor thing."

Sabie nodded politely and padded back inside.

"There's a lady back there who thinks I'm your granddaughter," she said, chuckling as she entered the living room.

Estelle spat onto her carpet. "Sheryl! Phah! If you were my granddaughter, I'd twist your ear this minute. Stealing from me that way, your own flesh and blood!"

"Hey, don't worry, I'm not Sheryl," Sabie said, throwing up her hands. For a moment it looked as though Estelle was going to have a stroke, her face knotted together so tightly. Then it slowly unfolded and she stared at Sabie consideringly.

"You're not running away from the police," she murmured, musingly.

"No." Sabie shook her head, not really paying attention. There were black things hanging from the ceiling. Thick and droopy, like old stage curtains. Could they really be spider webs?

"You're not old enough to be on your own. Even with my old eyes, I can see that."

Sabie ran her thumb under Ginny's collar, lifting the scratchy fabric away from her neck. She pretended not to hear.

"Well, in that case," said Estelle, fixing her faded blue eyes on her visitor. "Who are you, then?"

Chapter Six

Who was she? It was hard to say, really. A long time ago, she had been Sabie Pincher, a child with a mother at home and a father who sometimes visited. Then she had been Sabie Dulcimer, Sabie Shining, Sabie Singer, and, finally, Sabie Starr. Monika had always picked their names, whenever they had to move on. Once Sabie had wanted to pick "Cher" and Monika had laughed and said okay, she'd be Sonny, but when she'd given their names for the baby-sitting job, Monika had put down Sabina and Viola Dulcimer.

Would she go on being Sabie Starr forever and ever? Was she back to being Sabie Pincher, even though her old life was so long ago that it hardly belonged to her any more? Or could she be whoever she wanted to be, finally?

Estelle was waiting.

"I'm Sabie," Sabie mumbled, looking at her fingers.

Estelle grasped the handle of her cane and leaned forward. Even though she was sitting, her hand trembled on the cane. The loose skin of her face was so pale it reminded Sabie of a popped white balloon, the kind they hand out free at Safeway, the kind that she and Monika used to tie to little driftwood boats and sail in English Bay.

"You must think I'm a crazy old woman," Estelle murmured. "And maybe I am." Reaching under the worn, overstuffed cushion she was sitting on, she pulled out a grey ball of Kleenex and, with difficulty, peeled off a bit to dab her nose with. She wasn't very big, Sabie realized suddenly. For a grown-up.

Estelle tucked the used bit of tissue into the ankle of her sock. Then she looked at Sabie again. "You can help me," she said unexpectedly. "My devil daughter-in-law, Candace, is going to send her children back here to rob me again. She thinks that since Morty is dead, everything is hers. She's going to drive me into an early grave! She's been trying to for years. The doctor once gave me blood pressure pills to take just for thinking about her!"

As the old woman paused a moment, fumbling with some sofa crumbs, Sabie could hear her breath rattling in her throat like grains of rice in a box. But Estelle seemed more preoccupied with her relatives than her health. "Morty was always too good for her, you know. The first day he brought her home, I could see from her snake eyes that she had a demon in her."

Estelle tried to prop her cane up against the sofa

arm, but it slid to the ground. She retrieved it. "Morty said I was against her because she isn't Jewish. Hah! Snake eyes are snake eyes, and she has them. Wouldn't matter if she were a unicorn."

Sabie wasn't interested in Estelle's meanderings. She was worrying over where she would go now, wondering whether she should try that great evergreen on Cambie Street with the overhanging branches that she and Monika had slept in last year. Or that ancient treehouse in the alley off Granville Street. Maybe she could pinch a blanket from Estelle's basement; the old woman would never even miss it.

But it was too late to stop Estelle, who gripped her memories as tightly as she gripped her cane. "She treated me like vermin!" Estelle's voice blared, drawing Sabie's reluctant attention. "I don't know what went wrong between her and Morty. Morty was always too good for her, that's all I know. She threw him out and after that he was no good for anything. His heart was broken, he came to live with me. But what did their troubles have to do with me? I would have been the best grandma — the best. But she poisoned those kids against me. Poisoned them! And now they're just as bad as she is!"

Estelle trembled. Sabie felt like she'd been watching something private. She looked away.

"Maybe this is too much *kvetching* for a young girl," Estelle said, rising from the sofa with the help of her cane. "Come, we both need a little something."

Sabie followed the bent back across the room and into the tiny kitchen. "A little something" turned out to be Sanka and graham crackers from a box that had been left open too long.

Sabie looked out the window at Chateau Chrysler a little wistfully. She was going to miss it.

"A car is not a home," Estelle said, sitting across from her at the arborite-and-chrome table wedged between the fridge and the doorway. "Those cars in back, Morty was saving them for scrap."

Sabie took another cracker from the box. They were good soaked in Sanka, mushy and dark.

"You think people should just take what they want?" Estelle asked, her lips trembling as they drew together for a sip.

"Huh?" Sabie asked, startled. A guilty heat spread across her hairline. She had just been wondering whether the old woman would miss a few boxes of crackers along with the blanket.

But Estelle, as always, seemed to be talking mostly to herself. Sabie had the feeling that the woman would have had the same conversation with Henry, if the dog instead of Sabie had happened to be occupying the spare chair.

"They treated their father like dirt," Estelle said, as Sabie dunked another graham. "They made his last days miserable. Sure, I could open the doors and let them help themselves. But that would be like letting them spit on Morty's grave. I can't make peace with them now."

Sabie listened with interest as Estelle struggled to keep control of her voice. Monika's voice had always gone thin and wobbly like that when she spoke of Colin. Monika never could talk about Colin in the same light tone she used for other people who had once been part of their lives. When Sabie was younger, she had heard Monika's Colin voice come out of her own throat when she'd bitten down hard on her tongue and was trying to keep the tears from coming.

A dunked graham curled heavily over Sabie's finger, then dropped with a plop into her cup. She looked up to see if Estelle was annoyed that she had splashed the Sanka on the table, and was alarmed to find that the folds of the old woman's face were drawing downwards, not in annoyance, but as if she had soaked up more sorrow than she could hold.

A helicopter passed overhead, shaking the windows. Estelle placed her finger on the top of her cup, stopping its rattle. Then she murmured, "Sometimes you die before you find a way to fix things."

What was Estelle trying to fix? Sabie wondered. While she'd been thinking of Monika she had lost track of the old woman's worries. Suddenly she saw the two of them as they would have looked to a passerby: the worn, elderly woman, sucking her loose teeth as she talked of her dead son, and the scrawny girl wearing an outsized old dress and playing with her grahams.

"Me and Monika," Sabie said, faltering for a moment at having revealed her mother's name, "Well, sometimes one of us would get pretty sad. And when I got sad, Monika would play 'Don't Cry For Me, Argentina' on her guitar, but she'd make up really corny lyrics that always made me laugh. Like this . . ." Sabie sang, "Dry off your tears, little Sabie — You know that I always loved you. Although our roof leaks, although the rats squeak, we stick together . . . Now and forever!"

Estelle pulled at a bit of sweater wool with her crooked fingers. "I don't sing. It wouldn't be right, my only son in the grave."

Her voice was full of emptiness. She was holding out the emptiness, waiting for Sabie to fill it. Sabie felt that, and saw that a simple hug was probably all that Estelle wanted. But Sabie looked at Estelle's shoulder blades poking through her dirty sweater, thin and brittle-seeming as melba toast, and didn't think she could touch her. Sabie had enough sorrow of her own.

After a moment she went out the front door and around back to Chateau Chrysler. Retrieving her backpack, she carried it in to the house. She found Estelle in the living room, sitting expectantly on the sofa.

Sabie untied the backpack and drew out the violin. She spent a moment applying rosin to the bow and tuning the strings. But not too long. She noticed that Estelle's eyes had closed.

Slow and sweet, the music filled the room. At first, Sabie's mind was on Estelle, then on the cool curve of the chin rest against her cheek and the press of the strings against her fingers. Finally she lost herself in the music, in the bend and flow of it, and found the sound turning in on itself in the small room and in her heart, rushing like water to fill a hole. She played a long time before she realized that the music was searching for Monika, for Monika's fingers on the guitar, for Monika's voice stretched out in song. Monika had always led them musically; it was her mood that guided their selection of pieces, their tempo.

She lowered her violin.

"Beautiful," breathed Estelle. "Like a rainbow. And from a toy like that!"

Sabie smiled down at the small violin. "It does look sort of like a toy," she said. "I probably should have a full-sized one by now." You were supposed to get bigger violins as you grew. Monika had just never had the money. "Music like that could sweeten anybody," said Estelle, "anybody but Candace, of course. She's past anything good."

"Mm-hmm," murmured Sabie, setting her violin back in its case. Seemed like, no matter what, everything led back to Candace around here.

"That devil told Social Services about me," grumbled Estelle. "She wants them to put me in the Louis Brier Home with all those old people. Told them I can't look after myself."

Sabie looked around the living room, at the junk that stood in piles everywhere, at the carpets matted with dog hair, at the mousetraps that were scattered here and there. She didn't think Estelle could look after herself, either. If it were up to her, she'd send Estelle to an old folks' home too. But she kept her mouth shut. She and Estelle didn't have much in common, but Sabie knew what it felt like to fear people who could make decisions about your life for you. She and Monika had fought for their freedom; she guessed Estelle had a right to fight for hers too.

"I *kvetch* too much," admitted Estelle. "But you get old, you *kvetch*. There's so much to complain about. You wake up thinking it's going to be like the old days, but every day is the same — it's like someone put sand in the oatmeal."

Estelle pulled at her dress in rumination. Minutes passed. Sabie's thoughts began to drift. Her shoulder could still feel the pressure of the violin. She could almost smell the salt air of her old busking haunts and hear the guitar strings squeak under Monika's sliding fingers.

"All my life, I've had bad luck," volunteered Estelle, from the depths of the sofa. "A bad husband. An unlucky son. A devil for a daughter-in-law. And still I went to the synagogue, and still I kept kosher. Well, almost. And always I asked, 'Why is my life so bad if I am doing everything right?' And now, finally God has noticed me."

"Really?" Sabie blinked sleepily. Had she missed something?

"Yes," said Estelle, with conviction. "God sent you."

"Look," said Sabie, feeling that honesty in this case might be the best policy. "God couldn't have sent me. I don't believe in God."

"You have a lot in common with those blueberry bushes in my back yard. They don't believe in God either," said Estelle, a light springing into her faded eyes. "But Morty used to buy my milk. All the milk in the fridge is sour, and now you're here to buy milk for me. Explain that!"

Limping, she made her way to a chair and pushed its pile of yellowing newspapers onto the floor. As Sabie watched in amazement, Estelle drew her purse from under the seat cushion. There were all kinds of things under that cushion. Did Estelle think that thieves wouldn't look there?

Estelle drew three brown envelopes from her purse. "These are my pension cheques," she said, her voice cracking. "Morty used to cash them for me. The bank is right next to Safeway. You can deposit them there, then pick up some milk. Get two bottles."

"But you don't even know me!" exclaimed Sabie, looking at the cheques in her hand.

"Oh, I know you," said Estelle with a funny smile. "I know that you live in my car. So you will come back. Tell the bank you're my sister Ginny's grandchild, that you're staying with me. If they ask. But will they ask? They won't ask. They haven't asked me anything since they brought in those young tellers in nineteen eighty-two. I don't think any of them speak English, anyway. Or maybe they think all old ladies are deaf."

The air outside was hot and clean. Estelle's dry lawn gave off a sweet hay smell. Sabie was already at the curb when Estelle called her.

"Girl-l-l! Sabie-e-e!"

Sabie spun around and felt Ginny's dress slap against her calves. What was she doing outside in this crazy outfit?

The old woman was on her hands and knees

again, peering around the screen door at her.

The door opened a little wider. "Ginny married a Hoffman, Solly Hoffman. So you're Sabie Hoffman. Can you remember? Sabie Hoffman."

A flatbed truck carrying a backhoe turned off Cambie and rattled down Carr Avenue, belching oily smoke as it shifted gears. A motorcycle swerved around the truck, its swimsuit-clad driver steering with one hand as he used the other to help his passenger grip a surfboard. "Hi-YE-E-E!" the motorcyclists shouted at Sabie as they sped away.

Wondering at the different lives people lead, Sabie Hoffman, wearing Ginny Hoffman's best dress, trudged along the hot sidewalk to Safeway.

Chapter Seven

When Sabie returned from Safeway, she found Estelle sitting in the hallway on a stack of newspapers, puffing as if she had just completed a major archaeological dig. As she practically had, Sabie thought, for Estelle had moved enough papers to reveal a doorway Sabie had not noticed before. Through it, Sabie could see a wide bed surrounded by chairs and boxes.

"You'll sleep here," Estelle said, as if moving in was part of a plan they had already agreed upon. "It was Morty's room. I don't go in."

Estelle stared into the room contemplatively for a moment, her hands folded across the crook of her cane. Then she turned her gaze to Sabie. "You buried Henry for me. That's something those girls Social Services sent me would never do; they'd just pretend to dust and then tell the social worker I should live in a home. *Feh!*

You can stay; them I can do without."

The offer was unexpected. Sabie hesitated, scratching an old scab on her leg to give herself a little time. She knew Monika would want her to score the site, the way she'd scored Chateau Chrysler. She tried to focus on that: ten points for the bed, ten for the crackers and peanut butter in the basement. But she couldn't. After the fresh air and sunshine of her errand, the heat and old-lady smell of Estelle's house came at her like truck exhaust. The whole place had a cramped, greasy, dog-bowl feel to it that gummed up her thinking.

"What's to think about?" Estelle asked stridently. The mole above her eyebrow twitched. Suddenly Sabie could hear Monika whisper in her ear, *"Don't trust her. She's dangerous. Run!"*

"No!" Sabie blurted. Pivoting, she slipped on a bit of newspaper and threw her hand out against the wall for balance. Without looking back at the old woman who was sitting on the stack of papers, she hurried through the utility room to the porch and snatched her stiffened clothes from the railing. She couldn't wait to take off Ginny's ridiculous dress and get out.

Estelle came into the utility room just as Sabie was cramming Ginny's clothes into the green plastic bag.

"You would think I was putting your fingers into the fire, the kind of thanks you gave me," said the old woman. But her voice was mild. "Put that bag in the front closet. I did enough damage to myself getting it here."

Sabie did as instructed, relishing the clean, wrinkly feeling of her own clothes.

Estelle waited until Sabie had her hand on the handle of the front door before she called down the hallway, "Stay in the car if you're like that. But as long as you're in my backyard it wouldn't kill you to lift a finger to help now and then . . . "

"'Bye," Sabie said for politeness sake, and let the screen door swing shut with a bang. She went to the back, grabbed her stuff, and ran.

But that evening, she did return to the car to sleep, half-hoping Estelle wouldn't even notice. In the middle of the night, the noise of a helicopter landing at Children's Hospital woke her. She'd been pulled from a dream in which Monika's blanket-covered form on the ambulance stretcher, the dead dog Henry, and Estelle were all mixed up in some horrible way, and she found herself staring at the ceiling of Chateau Chrysler, unable to sleep. The slow beating of the helicopter's blades as it waited on the landing pad pulsed through the sleeping neighbourhood.

She felt unbearably alone. More so than at any other moment since Monika's death. She noticed the ordinary night smells of moist grass and far-away skunk, but the remnants of her dream made the usually cozy confines of Chateau Chrysler loom out of the dark in a cold and alien way. What was she doing, lying here in some old woman's rusting car, while around her children slept or were airlifted to hospitals under their parents' watchful eyes?

With Monika, Chateau Chrysler would have

been a castle, a cave, an island, a political statement, anything that they wished it to be. They would have awakened together with the helicopter's landing and whispered in the dark. Monika could transform a minor irritation into a captivating adventure, simply by applying her imagination with relish. But Monika's imagination, wherever it was now, wasn't strong enough to cross over the barrier of death to work its usual magic for her daughter alone.

Sabie slipped soundlessly out of the car and parted the long grass to sit, arms around knees, back against a cool tire, and stare at the stars. As a small child, waiting in the pickup for one of Blue Karma's late-night gigs to end, she'd often heard the stars whispering to her with their comforting cricket voices. Now, as she sat listening to the sky, the same night sky that had watched as her family had dwindled from three, to two, to one, she heard nothing but the soft groan of the elm's heavy limbs and the rushing of a bus's tires along Cambie.

Could she go on without Monika? No, not go on; she didn't mean that. Of course she would go on. But, could one person be a family? Had Monika ever looked ahead and wondered that? Could Monika's magic continue without Monika?

A raccoon emerged from the tangle of blueberry bushes and waddled across Henry's fresh grave. Sabie watched the animal disappear alongside Estelle's house and wondered if Estelle, inside, was dreaming of Morty.

When the sky had the same silty brightness as dew on the Chrysler's dusty hood, Sabie stood and stretched and acknowledged that she had a new, unforeseen hunger. Not a hunger for crisp celery or blueberry danishes or spicy balls of falafel, or any of the other tempting foods that were rare treats in her life with Monika, but a hunger to be with someone who had known Monika. Someone who knew Sabie, the real Sabie.

Sabie needed to find Parker.

Monika had had a rule about friends. Find 'em, taste 'em, turf 'em, she'd summed it up to Sabie. Every friendship is unique and valuable, she'd said, but dangerous. So Sabie, though she longed for a real best friend, made do with friendships that lasted no longer than an afternoon at the library or beach.

When she was younger, that had meant a day of building driftwood castles on the beach, sharing lunch, with a shrug and a goodbye wave when asked for her phone number or which school she went to. More recently, Sabie had been drawn to kids in crisis. A chance encounter with a bleak-faced teenager hunched over a stack of books on divorce or pregnancy frequently led to long and delicious discussions about how unfair it is that parents have all the power, or just what a seventeen-year-old has to do to be a good parent. Sabie savoured these heart-to-hearts but, like Cinderella's ball gown, the fairytale friendships evaporated all too soon.

Parker was the one exception to Monika's rule. There was nobody like him. A one-legged mandolin player who drank heavily and was about to lose his other leg to diabetes, he'd known Monika since before Colin and Blue Karma. There had never been any need to hide from Parker because, like Monika and Sabie, Parker didn't officially exist. Escaping from some bad memory, he'd snuck into Canada twenty years earlier in a tourist's station wagon and had simply stayed, busking and living in shared apartments or under the Burrard Street Bridge, depending on his fortunes. He'd never minded sharing his haul when Monika and Sabie didn't have enough for coffee. While he wasn't exactly dependable, he was more constant than anything in Sabie's life, except Monika.

Sabie gathered her violin and backpack and made her way to Granville Island, Parker's favourite good-weather busking haunt. It was still so early, most stores weren't open yet; storefronts had a freshly-scrubbed expectancy, like a row of movie extras. Mostly, Sabie chose the side streets, where newspapers in their elastic bands waited on doorsteps and mist rose off lawns in the morning sun.

She got there hours too soon, of course. Parker never showed up anywhere until noon. But she waited on the pier, dangling her legs over the barnacle-encrusted pilings, and watched schools of small fish dart in and out of the shadows while all around her trucks unloaded their boxes of fresh vegetables and fruit.

"Morning, kid," called out one of the unicyclists who were setting up for a show in a roped-off cobblestone triangle. Crowds were already gathering, drawn by their colourful hats and assortment of cycles.

"Hi," she answered shyly. She'd watched his act many times.

"Where's your mom?" the cyclist asked, mounting a small unicycle and cycling a loop around Sabie. "We could go for some backup here."

"Oh, around," replied Sabie vaguely, managing a smile as she backed away. "Catch you later."

She busked a little, just long enough to buy herself a fresh baguette and a bag of overripe cherries, then she found Parker setting up farther along the pier, near the parking area.

"Hey, Sabe," he said, when he saw her. "Why don't you guys come and jam a while?"

Suddenly, she didn't know what to say. So she stood and watched while Parker plucked away at a tune, his black wide-brimmed hat shading his face so that the sun caught only the bottom wedge of his chin. There was more white in his stubble than she remembered.

A couple of minutes into the melody, Parker looked up and met Sabie's eyes. Immediately his fingers stilled over the mandolin and he patted the ground next to him. "Set yourself down here, girl," he said. "Talk to me."

Sabie lowered herself slowly onto the rough-hewn plank and held the backpack with her violin in it to her chest. People stepped around them, but she kept her eyes to the ground.

When she was finally able to bring herself to speak the words, she said them simply: "Mom died."

He drew in his breath sharply, then his broad hand slipped around her shoulders and drew her tightly against him. She felt the smooth sheety feel of his shirt against her cheek and smelled the musky old-wine and sweat smell of him. It was nothing like Monika, and with a stab of pain she knew again that Monika was not coming back. But the beat of Parker's heart in his barrel chest was steady and reassuring.

"Wish I could take you in or something," he said after she'd told him her story. "But you know I can't."

"I know," she said.

They sat silently awhile, Parker's arm still awkwardly around her.

"You need to say goodbye," he said.

"How?" asked Sabie. She had no body to bury and no place to bury it. "I don't want to say goodbye. I want to have her back!" she cried. She knew she sounded like a whining child, but she couldn't help it.

Parker used his crutches to lever himself to a stand. The tide had come in and the water was slick and black.

"What does this place make you think of?" he asked.

She looked around at the pigeon droppings and the clusters of people hunched over *lattes* or fries. She'd been here hundreds of times with Monika.

"I don't know," she said.

Parker laughed. "It makes me think of the time me and Monika were sitting here singing our hearts out with hardly anything but nickels to show for it, when some guy walks over to you at that corner, there, and drops you a tenner just for tuning your fiddle. The sounds you were making could have put a cat hospital to shame."

Sabie shrugged. "Well, I was only eight," she said. She'd heard that story many times.

Parker heaved a mock sigh. "That's when I realized that cute wins over talent every time." He stood quietly for a moment. Then he said, "You going to keep on like Monika wanted you to, staying on your own and all?"

"I guess so," Sabie replied, watching a young woman snatch up a toddler who had wandered too near the edge of the pier.

"I don't know about those plans of hers," Parker said reflectively. "Never was too sure that was the right way to raise a kid. You might want to think about it a bit."

She squeezed her arms hard into her sides. "I'm not a kid any more," she reminded him.

"Guess you're right," he said, and there was a weariness in his voice that made her look up into his familiar, friendly, seamed face.

"So, how do I say goodbye?" she asked.

His dark eyes moved across the marina and back to her face. "I don't know as there's a good answer to that," he said. "A mother is the person who brings you into the world, who's a part of your every moment." He paused, rubbing his chest as though he'd been struck. "Once your mother's gone, it's like you're born into the world all new again. But this time, on your own feet."

Parker's words made Sabie think of Monika's dance with life, of dancing with Monika on the beach. "Parker," she whispered, "I'm not really sure if I can do this by myself."

Parker rubbed his chin. "I'm not good at this kind of talk," he told her. "How 'bout some cocoa?" He led her into the market building and ordered two cups of steaming chocolate from the pie stand. Sabie carried them to a table.

Parker settled heavily into a wooden chair. "I'm going to miss Monika," he said, clearing the hoarseness from his throaty big-city voice. "She was a darned good listener when you needed someone, you know?"

"I know," murmured Sabie, and squeezed her cup so hard she popped the lid off the styrofoam.

Parker snapped the lid back on for her. "Look at you," he said remorsefully. "I shouldn't be talking like this."

"It's all right," whispered Sabie, licking the chapped place on her lip. "But I don't think I'm ever going to stop missing her."

Parker set her hands around her cup and squeezed them gently. "No, you ain't. You ain't."

Exhaustion overtook Sabie. She thought longingly of Chateau Chrysler and sleep. That reminded her of something she wanted to talk to Parker about.

"Hey, Parker," she said. She meant to give him just the bare facts, but found herself telling him all about Estelle, Morty, even old Henry. She was amazed at the way Estelle's face was so clearly before her as she spoke; she could almost have mapped out the lines around the woman's eyes. "So, she invited me to stay with her," she finished. "What do you think?"

"I thought you said the house stinks," said Parker.

Sabie shrugged thoughtfully. "That's not the real problem. I could always clean it. But, like, what if Estelle calls the cops one day? What if she decides I should be in a foster home?"

Parker turned his foam cup between his fingers. "That's a problem you're always going to face," he told her. "And if it happens, you'll just have to deal with it then."

"I guess." Sabie picked at the varnished table-top with her fingernail. "But I don't think Monika would have wanted me to stay with Estelle. I don't think she'd want me to stay with *anybody*. That's not what she planned."

Parker pitched their empty cups into a nearby garbage can. "You're on your own two feet now. Making your own decisions is one way of saying goodbye."

A trio of chattering middle-aged women squeezed by them and carried away their unused chair. The market was filling up. Soon there would be people with trays of food in their hands looking longingly at Sabie and Parker's spot.

"So, what're you going to do?" Parker asked, gently.

Sabie shut her eyes and reached for an answer. Then she looked at Parker. "I'm going to give it a try with Estelle, I guess. For a few days, anyway. She didn't turn me in last night, and she could have."

"Are you almost finished here?" inquired a man holding a plate of steamed vegetables. Parker waved him away, but Sabie stood.

"We'd better get going." She handed Parker his crutches. "By the way," she said, "Are *you* going to do anything special to say goodbye to Monika?"

Parker smiled. "I don't have to. I can see a whole lot of her standing right in front of me."

Chapter Eight

So Sabie stayed; and for a cranky old lady, Estelle turned out to be full of surprises. Right after Sabie had washed Morty's sheets, brushed Henry's hair from the carpet, and shoved aside some of the canopy of junk, she discovered her eccentric landlady was a chess expert. Not just an expert, but a championship player.

"My husband was a no-good," Estelle told Sabie matter-of-factly by way of explanation. "No good around the house, no good at making money. I played chess to get away from him." She settled herself down on the sofa as Sabie pulled up a small table with a dusty chess board on it. Sabie found a rag and carefully wiped the board and pieces. They were large, heavy stone pieces, pink ones of Jerusalem stone, Estelle told her, and grey ones of Canadian Shield granite. Morty had made them for her before he married Candace.

Sabie lifted the grey queen from the board. It felt cold in her palm, colder than the room, and heavy for its size. This was a queen with a lot packed into her. "I'll be grey," Sabie said.

Estelle smiled. "Morty liked to play grey, too," she said, dropping a sofa cushion onto her pink-socked feet for warmth. "He said that any rock that survived being scoured by glaciers must have a lot of strength in it. But I like Jerusalem stone."

"Because you like pink?" asked Sabie.

"No, because it comes from a place that has seen so much trouble."

Sabie waited for further explanation, but when Estelle remained silent, tugging at her lip whiskers, Sabie asked, "So, what do you like about that?"

Estelle lifted the pink queen and pressed it into Sabie's hand so that Sabie could feel its sandy coolness. "It's soaked up so much trouble and sorrow, and hasn't been ground to sand," the old woman explained. Then, with what Sabie would almost have sworn was a grin (if she hadn't known that people that ancient were too old to grin) Estelle added, "Like me!"

Then Estelle lifted each piece from the board, running her gnarled fingers over their crudely-chiseled features. "How did playing chess get you away from your husband?" Sabie asked.

Estelle blew dust from a pink knight. "The competitions were never in small towns," she said. "I had to travel. Winnipeg. Regina. Montreal, once. Even Minneapolis. We didn't have any money, but the synagogue Sisterhood in Regina raised money for my bus fare. The Winnipeg paper — the Jewish one — wrote about me. How could my husband say no?"

When Estelle smiled and her skin drew smooth across her cheeks something shone from her that was — well, not young, Sabie admitted, but something that made the years between the two of them disappear. It was as if the age that was all over Estelle's body, in her hunched cane-tapping and in her crooked fingers, had disappeared into the smile, and the inner Estelle had emerged.

"I don't know much about chess," Sabie warned Estelle. Monika had taught her the basic moves — one of the places she'd worked as a baby-sitter had had a chess board in the living room — but she hadn't played since.

"Don't worry about what you know," Estelle reassured her. "You just let the pieces be themselves. You be their eyes, and let them do what they do. Don't think too much." Estelle chuckled when she saw Sabie's dubious look. "I know it's not what you hear about chess. You hear that it's a game for brains. Phah!" She tapped her chest, rattling the key pinned there. "It's a game from your heart. From inside. Listen to your queen, if she's afraid, if she wants to attack. Then do it. So what about the rook on the other side, or the bishop! Listen to your queen."

"My queen talks about as much as you'd expect from a rock," Sabie pointed out practically. "I think it would help if you went over the rules."

"Rules, shmules," said Estelle. "What we need

to start the game is chocolate. You never play chess without chocolate."

So Sabie had to run out to the corner store for some chocolate. After that, they played chess and ate chocolate at least once a day. Sabie learned some pretty sneaky moves — "That queen of yours, she's got a thing or two up her sleeve," Estelle teased her — but Estelle always won. Sabie taped coloured papers to the pieces so that Estelle could tell them apart easily. Blue for bishops, purple for pawns. "Yellow for kings," Estelle said, and when Sabie asked her why yellow, she turned her face away slyly and said, "They're always on the run."

Estelle also turned out to be a Cary Grant fan. Anytime there was a Cary Grant movie, everything stopped. The kettle was put on for tea, and the two of them curled up in front of the TV. Sabie quickly became a Cary Grant expert. It was her job to sniff out his movies by scanning a *TV Guide* at the Safeway checkout. Nineteen-forty was their favourite Cary Grant year; that was the year he did *The Philadelphia Story* and *His Girl Friday*.

"In nineteen-forty," mused Estelle, "I was a young mother, not the beauty of my family, but pretty enough to have my admirers, even then!"

Sabie was skeptical about the admirers. How could someone who was all nose and hardly any chin ever be beautiful, even without wrinkles?

Perhaps Estelle caught the skepticism in Sabie's silence, for she added, somewhat huffily, "I held up better than some, you know. Bluma Gottfried thought she was really something special, with that hourglass figure, but by the time she was fifty — well! There wasn't a girdle in the Sears catalogue that could swallow one of her thighs, let alone her waist!"

Gradually, Sabie got used to Estelle's crabbiness. She guessed that Estelle just didn't know how to say happy things; her pattern of talking had been set by a life of sad happenings. But underneath the scabbiness was a sharp humour and even warmth. Estelle, in some ways, was like a live volcano: rough crusty rock on the outside, hot bubbling stuff inside. This was not to be confused with the idea that Estelle was sweet or gentle at the core. There were sharp spurs that went right through her. Drawing near, you could get spiked on them. But only sometimes.

Some days Sabie was repulsed by the misshapen old woman who snored open-mouthed on the sofa and kept used Kleenex in her socks. But other days she found Estelle's eccentricities delicious. Estelle wasn't even embarrassed when Sabie first caught her peering across the street with binoculars.

"Do you know what happens if I don't watch?" she asked. She didn't wait for Sabie to answer. "See that house across the road? Two years ago their two-year-old got out of the house before six in the morning. Made a beeline for Cambie Street. It's only four houses to Cambie Street! He would have been — you don't even want to think about that. But I called his parents, got them out of bed."

"They must really have thanked you," Sabie

murmured, trying to scratch off the grey dust that seemed always to cling to her legs these days. Sometimes she felt like her skin couldn't breathe, it was clogged up with must and dust and dog hair.

"Thanked me! Thanked me! Sure they thanked me!" exclaimed Estelle. "They were all over me, sent flowers over. What do you think?"

"Why haven't they been around lately?" asked Sabie.

Estelle scowled. She turned her face into the binoculars and wouldn't answer. After a moment she waved Sabie over.

"Look across there," she said. "There's a man breaking in. Look, he's got a ladder. He's on the ladder — there, can you see? He's probably planning to go in a window and take things."

"I don't think someone would use a ladder to get into that house," Sabie answered, leaning across the worn sofa to peer across the street. "It would be easier to go through a basement window."

Estelle slapped Sabie's shoulder. "Think! Think!" she exclaimed. "If he breaks a window, we're going to call the police. No, he uses a ladder and we don't call the police. We think he's a house painter. Everybody thinks he's a house painter. Then he runs inside, steals the baby — "

"Carries the baby down the ladder?" Sabie couldn't suppress a giggle.

Estelle propped herself up awkwardly, pulling on Sabie's arm for help. "You don't know what can happen," she said. "Lindbergh's baby was carried down a ladder."

"Whose baby?" asked Sabie, unhooking Estelle's fingers from her bare arm. She hated it when Estelle grabbed her like that, either to help herself up or to make a point. Sabie herself avoided touching Estelle.

"And there was another baby, a Jewish baby in Point Grey, who was stolen a few years ago. Terrible thing. They never caught the murderer."

A police car moved down the street. Sabie was sure that the cop saw Estelle peering through the binoculars, but he didn't slow down even a little.

"Look at that! All the money we pay the police and they don't even check out what's going on with that ladder!" Estelle pushed a pillow up to rest her elbow on. She was as excited as a little kid in a roller coaster line-up, thought Sabie. The old woman squinted through the binoculars again. She got Sabie to help hold them because her bad arm was tiring.

"I told that Linda not to let the baby nap by an open window!" she said. "I warned her that one day some man with a ladder would come along and — "

"Look," said Sabie. "There's a truck out there. It says *CAMBIE INSULATION AND SIDING*. He's just doing his job."

"Maybe," said Estelle. "But do you think a baby thief wouldn't be smart enough to put a sign on his truck to keep us from worrying? Then, he goes around the corner a little, he throws the sign away, he's got the baby — "

"Why would anyone go to so much trouble to steal a baby?" asked Sabie. "You'd be way better off stealing a computer. They don't cry and need diapers!"

Estelle tapped her finger on Sabie's arm. "There are all kinds of baby rings," she said. "You're too young to know. Bring me the phone."

"Why?"

"Bring me the phone! At a time like this, you want to ask a million questions?"

Sabie brought the phone. It took her five minutes just to unravel the cord so that it could reach. Estelle grabbed it with shaking hands. She tapped out seven numbers.

"Hello? Who is this? Linda? What? Oh." She pulled her head away from the phone. "It's a baby-sitter," she said. "Listen, there's a man climbing up a ladder near the baby's room. You had better go and get the baby. Then find out who he is. If I see that man climbing in your window, I'm calling the police."

Sabie pushed her face so hard into a cushion to muffle her giggles that the dust made her sneeze. When she finally came up for air, still giggling and sneezing, Estelle was grinning at her.

"It was a workman," she said.

"Really?" Sabie managed to say. Her fingers were all pins and needles from the giggling.

Estelle didn't seem at all perturbed. "I'm calling the police anyway," she said. "Who takes the word of a teenager? You think a professional baby thief couldn't fool a teenager?"

Sabie looked at Estelle carefully. She felt a glimmer of suspicion that Estelle was not surprised that the workman was not a baby thief. In fact, she was beginning to wonder whether Estelle might not be trying to cause trouble with that family. "You're up to something," she said.

"Let's see how long it takes the police to come," Estelle replied, dialling. "Last time it was an hour."

"If you saved their kid from Cambie Street," Sabie asked again after Estelle had put down the phone, "how come they never come over?" She felt daring, wondering if Estelle would answer her this time, or snap at her and clam up.

Estelle shoved some old Home Hardware flyers under the sofa to straighten out the sag. "Dr. Meyers, he's the father, he took me to *shul* for a bit."

"And . . . ?"

The old woman's eyes sparked, something between humour and embarrassment. "I hit him."

"You *hit* him?"

Estelle leaned her cheek against the curve of her cane. Her eyes glinted around their cataracts. "He always wanted to take me to see some specialist. I didn't want to go. One day, he just drove me. I yelled at him to turn back. I wanted to go to *shul,* it was the Braverman *bar mitzvah*, the Bravermans are cousins of my dentist, anyway there was sure to be good food and lots of babies. He wouldn't listen. Just like I was a child. It made me so mad! I hit him!" She thwacked her cane on the floor.

"With your cane?" asked Sabie.

"A prayer book. Hardcover."

"Good."

Chapter Nine

"Do you really think Sheryl and Mark will come back?" Sabie asked one morning. She had just rigged a makeshift lock for Estelle's kitchen door. Just in case the two pieces of scum tried to slither up the stepless back staircase.

"Oh, yes," said Estelle, who was sitting, as always, on the sofa, the curtains closed behind her. One foot was drawn up onto her lap. "Of course they will. They'll try to get the rest before I sell it."

"*Will* you sell it?" asked Sabie, her eyes drawn against her will to the workings of Estelle's gnarled fingers. With disgusted fascination, Sabie watched as Estelle peeled a double layer of dirty socks over her heel to reveal a knobby, veined foot.

"Sell it?" barked Estelle. "And invite people inside my house to look at all this?" With a sweep of her good arm, she indicated the sofa, the curtains, the carpet. "This used to be a showcase," she said, "a model home. Those curtains are silk, not that you could guess. Before that *chazer* and his dog moved in and ruined it, I used to be proud to show it."

Sabie still hadn't got used to the way Estelle spoke about her son, how she could call him a pig when she loved him so much that she cried all the time. Didn't you either love someone or not?

"You could take everything to a second-hand shop," she suggested.

"What?" sputtered Estelle. "And *shlep* it around? I can't even carry a sandwich, let alone a TV. No, let it all sit here. When I die, the whole house will be bulldozed. It's in my will. That devil and her children won't get a penny." She let out a yelp. "Oh, Christopher Columbus, these feet will be the death of me yet!"

Sabie leaned over. "What are you doing?"

"What am I doing, she asks. What do you think I am doing? I'm getting ready to soak my feet, that's what I'm doing."

Sabie thought Estelle's foot looked as though it had melted like wax, oozed out in odd directions, and hardened again. It was even a waxy colour and not at all shoe-shaped.

"How come it looks like that?" Sabie couldn't help asking.

Estelle grimaced as she put her foot down and pulled the other one onto her lap. "They're just old-lady feet," she said. "With bunions. Make sure you wear the right size shoes so you don't end up with feet like these. Bunions make walking feel like there are teeth in your shoes."

"I thought you had arthritis," said Sabie. Didn't all old people have arthritis or rheumatism? Wasn't that why Estelle had been hobbling?

"Arthritis!" guffawed Estelle. "Ginny had arthritis. Arthritis is a bubble bath compared to what I have."

"Bunions?"

"Parkinson's," declared Estelle, almost triumphantly. She dropped the second clump of dirty socks beside her and it lay stiffly, holding its foot shape.

"Parkinson's and hardening of the arteries and high blood pressure. That's what Dr. Klein told me years ago, and I've been battling it ever since. I'm going blind because of hardening of the arteries. And the Parkinson's makes me shake. He told me it might affect my mind, but I've got my mother's mind. Sharp like a letter opener."

"Why don't you let your doctor fix your feet, at least?" asked Sabie, wiggling her own toes and feeling glad at the ordinary toeness of them.

"That devil, Candace, has him wrapped around her snaky little finger," muttered Estelle. "He'd help her put me in a home if he got a chance. Anyway, Morty used to drive me there. How would I get there now?"

Sabie remembered how Monika had avoided doctors, too. Instead, she'd tried something called homeopathy, and visited sweatlodges and healing circles. She'd even taught Sabie how to do a special kind of massage.

Personally, Sabie liked doctors. Before she and

Monika had run away Sabie had gone to a doctor in a shopping mall who had listened carefully to her complaints, made her better, and seen to it that she had a purple helium-filled balloon whenever she left.

"The back door's locked now," said Sabie, switching the subject. "Sheryl and Mark can bring their crowbars, doesn't matter, they won't get in."

"Cockroaches don't need crowbars."

"So, what's next? Want to play chess?" Sabie suggested. She was becoming a bit of a chess fan herself.

Estelle sucked her dentures for a moment, considering. Then she came up with another suggestion. "Why don't you shut up the basement windows? Nail them closed."

"Hey, why didn't I think of that?" Sabie teased. "What a fun way to spend a hot, sunny day!"

Estelle returned her smile. "You think the rabbits are loose upstairs," she said, patting her wiry white hair that could not be tamed by hairpins. "But I'm not crazy, I'm just old. My bones tell me things. They tell me trouble is coming. And what could that trouble be, but my grandchildren? Now, bring me a bowl of hot water for my feet."

So Sabie found herself spending the next few days in the basement, building a Mark-and-Sheryl-proof fortress. She was quite good at it, actually. Fortress-building was a form of carpentry that allowed a lot of free expression, and Sabie was sure Monika would have loved it.

First Sabie attached the slatted wooden sides of

a playpen across the small windows. For good measure she nailed the ragged curtains shut too, hoping fervently that she never had to get out of the basement in a hurry. Then she nailed a picnic table bench across the door.

The basement was jammed to the ceiling with fascinating stuff. She began making a list of all the things that were down there. It was unlikely that Estelle would ever be able to make it down the steep, banisterless stairs to investigate. Maybe when she learned what Morty had stockpiled, she would be more than happy to let people take anything they wanted.

It was obvious that over the years Morty had spent a lot of time buying things for his children. Sabie guessed that Candace hadn't let him give the children anything and all of it had ended up entombed in Estelle's basement. There were ice skates that had never been worn, an inflatable swimming pool gone brittle in its package, a Popeye punching bag — things that Mark and Sheryl were far too old to use now.

Morty had also been a garage sale nut and a hoarder. In one damp corner were six rusty lawn mowers and eleven ancient televisions. (Eleven! Sabie marvelled.) In another, bumping up against the coarse cedar joists, was a cluster of curve-topped fridges and battered electric frying pans. There were two quaint-looking Osborne computers and several boxes of musty coats.

A couple of little kids could have a great time here, Sabie thought one afternoon as she noted down "112 empty 7-UP bottles." You could build a really great hideout, a hundred great hideouts. You could stick secret messages in the 7-UP bottles and throw them off the Burrard Bridge into the inlet. Maybe one would be turned up by a fisherman's daughter in Japan, and you could become pen pals.

Sabie had never seen so many possessions in one place. Since she and Monika had moved a lot, they owned only what could be carried on their backs. But she began to wonder whether Colin was like Morty, a collector of things. Her memories of Colin were dim, but why else would Colin have gone off with Other Woman but to enjoy her mansion, her Mercedes, her CDs, notebook computer and all the other treasures she and Monika imagined had been used to lure Colin away from them?

Soaking up Morty with the must and the mess, Sabie felt that she was also beginning to understand Colin. If Colin was like Morty, with an overpowering desire to fill his life up with things, then no wonder he hadn't been able to stay with Monika, who held onto nothing but her music and her child.

On her third afternoon in the basement Sabie found herself leaning against the cool, smooth door of a Frigidaire, cheek and chest pressed flat, eyes shut, imagining that she was Colin, loving clutter, comforted by crowding, needing to *own* . . . She moulded herself to the enameled curve of the Fridgidaire, remembering how she used to play with Colin's glasses, how their lenses had curved coolly like this door. She'd sat on his lap, chewing the stems. Funny, she had forgotten that — never thought of it even once in all these years! — and yet now she could remember exactly how the glasses' earpiece had tasted, a warm vinyl that stung her tongue.

Did Colin have any memories of Sabie, she wondered, that were as clear as that?

Abruptly Sabie became aware of how low the ceiling was with its web-choked beams, and of the fishy smell of unwashed dog food tins. It was a basement of things left behind by a dead person, things that had no meaning to anybody. She, the left-behind daughter, did not want to stand in it and think of her father.

"Here's your list," she called, taking the stairs two at a time, then slapping the paper down on the sofa cushion next to Estelle. "It's gross down there! I'm never going down there again."

Estelle set her binoculars onto the window ledge and manouevred around to peer at Sabie. "You sound just like Ginny. She hated going to the cellar for potatoes."

Sabie hung her thumbs on the elastic waistband of her shorts. She felt antsy for some reason, too antsy to sit down. Her clothes were itchy. Her skin was itchy. Even the bones of her hips felt itchy. "Well, I'm not Ginny. I'm just a kid," she reminded Estelle grumpily.

Estelle smiled. "Ginny was just a kid, too. Our mother used to send her down into the cellar for potatoes to make a special kind of pancake — "

Sabie groaned. "It's too hot to talk about Ginny," she said. "I've just spent three days in the basement. Did you know you have rats down there?"

"I don't have rats."

"Yes, you do. I saw two. And rat poo."

"*I* don't have rats," Estelle repeated, stressing the "I." "Morty does. That's his stuff down there."

Sabie nudged a mousetrap with her sandal; it sprang, doing a neat acrobatic flip with its bait. "A little trap like this isn't going to catch those big guys."

"I don't want to catch any rats," claimed Estelle, wrinkling her nose so that the straw-like hairs on her lip stood out. "A bunch of dead rats lying around, that's all I need!"

Sabie picked up the front page of the *Sun*, sighed, put it down, and picked up an old *TV Guide*.

"You have *shpilkes*," Estelle volunteered, observing her. "Morty used to get like that. He'd dance around that way, like a drop of water in a frying pan. Why don't you go out and get some sun?"

"It's raining," Sabie complained. "I was downstairs the whole time it was sunny."

"So it's raining. Since when do you let that stop you?" Estelle picked up her binoculars and parted the curtains.

Sabie didn't know what she wanted, or why she felt the way she did. She'd been enjoying making the list, and now, for no reason at all, she wished she were climbing a mountain somewhere. Only she felt too crabby to go out the front door, let alone find a mountain to climb.

"It's really bad to have rats," she said, pushing

her finger through the dust on the television.

"Eh?"

"If they're down in the basement, they're probably up here too. On the table, eating crackers."

"Good for them," said Estelle.

"You know, we should just give Mark and
Sheryl a call and tell them to come and pick the stuff
up." Sabie was looking at a picture of Morty when
he was three: chubby-cheeked, squinty-eyed, in
shorts. She tipped it over, face down.

Estelle set her binoculars down firmly, and
turned back to face Sabie. One pink-socked foot hit
the carpet as she turned, and she grimaced.

"Oh, I knew it, I was waiting for it," she said
between her teeth, cradling her foot in her hand.

Hearing the crankiness in Estelle's voice,
Sabie's own irritability vanished. "What's wrong,
your bunions?" she asked. Estelle kneaded her foot
through the sock. "No, not my bunions," she
snapped. "My feet I live with every day of my life.
What's to wait for?" She set her foot down gingerly.
"No, I was waiting for you to hurt me."

"Hurt you!" Sabie exclaimed, taken aback. "I
wouldn't do that!"

"Oh, sit down! I hate to see you hovering like
that!" Estelle dislodged newspapers from a chair
with her cane and waved Sabie into it.

Sabie sat. The emotional teeter-totter she and
Estelle seemed to be on had suddenly dumped her
down again.

The old woman sank into the sofa's ample cushions. "I saw the way you were dancing, not doing

74

this, not doing that, not sitting, not standing. Something with claws was riding your shoulders."

"Huh?"

Estelle adjusted her sweater. "Morty got that way when something had him in its claws. On Father's Day, on birthdays, he would stay near the phone, dancing, waiting to see if Mark and Sheryl would call."

"They probably didn't, much," Sabie guessed.

"They didn't, ever," Estelle agreed, emphatically. "And all day long, Morty would get that look, the look that you just had. The pain was too much for him. Then he would hit me."

"What?" Sabie exclaimed. Then, stupidly, "But he was your son!"

Estelle's cheek twitched, and she rubbed it with the back of her hand. "He was here, I was here, I was the one he hit. He never meant it to be hard, but I broke my wrist falling once," she said, holding out one thin, misshapen arm for Sabie to inspect.

Sabie crossed to the sofa and bent down to look at the wrist, seeing a knob that shouldn't be there, a knob that couldn't be hidden by the dry, loose skin. "That's awful!" she said. "Why did he do it?"

Estelle pulled her wrist back and drew her sleeve over it. "He couldn't take his pain, what Candace did to him, so it would build up in him until he hit me. It just happened." She pulled a tissue from her sleeve to wipe her nose, and Sabie saw with concern that the old woman's eyes had gone pink.

"Hey . . . " she murmured.

Estelle squeezed the tissue into a ball and

worked it with her fingers. "It's a funny thing, families," she said. "Love, hate, it's a pudding all cooked together. My Morty, I boiled his diapers on the stove when he was a baby, I keep his first tooth in a Gerber's jar, I'm so mad at him I can't sleep at night, but I'm still his mother."

Sabie pulled a cushion onto her lap and hugged it. She didn't know what to say, so she said nothing. She thought of the way Estelle spoke of Morty, sometimes with grief, sometimes pride, sometimes anger. How could a mother be so mixed up? Especially such an old mother. Kids were supposed to be the mixed-up ones.

And even if Estelle was Morty's mother, how could she love him even one little bit after what he he'd done to her? After all, he wasn't a little kid, just learning. He was past fifty when he died, bald, a loser with a stinky dog. You couldn't be a mother to a guy like that. By the time you got so old, didn't motherness dry up?

"Anyway," Sabie said firmly, "I would never hit you."

Estelle plucked at Sabie's shoulder and leaned toward her, so close that Sabie could feel Estelle's warm, herring breath on her face. She looked down.

"Hit me, no," Estelle said. "But hurt me, yes. What you said, to call Mark and Sheryl, that was like a poke in the eye."

Sabie flushed. She picked at her knee.

Estelle patted her shoulder gently. "Don't worry, it's not so bad. You're not breaking my wrist and, anyway, a wrist is not a heart. But something has its claws into you. What is it?"

Sabie felt like she couldn't breathe. Estelle was much too close. She stood up, pretending to have to scratch her back.

Estelle watched her for a moment. "Okay, so don't tell," she said.

Sabie scuffed the carpet with her toe, dislodging a flake of cracker. "It's just the stuff in the basement," she answered. "Just all that stuff, that's all."

"Just stuff?" echoed Estelle. "That's easy then. I wish my problems were just stuff. Take your fiddle, there, and go out in the fresh air and play."

Chapter Ten

Sabie took Estelle's advice and went to Granville Island. Granville Island was always a good busking bet, and now that the brief sun shower had ended there was bound to be a crowd of tourists flocking to the market. What could do a better job of raising Sabie's spirits than a pocketful of loonies and bills?

On the way she mulled over what Estelle had told her about Morty. Something about it weighed on her, but she wasn't quite sure what. Monika kept slipping into the Morty-and-Estelle mixture, but why? Monika wasn't at all like Estelle, and Sabie wasn't like Morty.

Finally she concluded that the heavy feeling didn't come from anything Estelle had said at all, but just from being closed in a musty old house for so long, thinking about Estelle's crazy relatives. The air outside was so clean and light she felt like she was floating as she walked. It was the same super-light feeling she used to get at the roller rink after taking off a pair of heavy skates and slipping into her sneakers. The rain-soaked pavement was steaming in the sun, making an earthy, wet-poolside-cement smell. If Monika were alive, Sabie thought wistfully, they would be at Kits Beach right now, writing tide-poetry in the damp sand.

By the time she got to Granville Island there were many buskers already set up. Some of them, like the juggler and the guitarist, had permits. She could tell by the spots they held, and by their photo IDs . The Market wasn't like the strip or Broadway, where you could pretty much just squat and play. It was watched. But here and there she could see an unpermitted busker standing discreetly under a bridge pillar or sitting on the grass.

"Hey, Sabie," drawled a familiar voice. She turned and saw Parker, who had set up in the triangle of concrete where two roads converged. "Long time, no see. How goes the battle?"

"Hey, Parker," replied Sabie, grinning as a rush of affection for his worn face washed over her, though she could tell by his soiled clothes and trembling hands that he'd been on a drinking binge. Pulling off her backpack, she leaned against the concrete, one leg propped up behind her. "Hanging in there. Same old same old."

Parker fumbled with the strings of his mando-lin. "Same old same old?" he echoed. "I don't think so. Talk to me, girl."

Parker looked ill and his playing was off. Sabie knew he was in a bad way.

"I'm hanging in pretty good," she told him. "That place I told you about? Could be worse."

Parker nodded. He picked up the cottage cheese container he was using to collect money and gave it a shake as he peered into it.

"Oughta be 'bout enough," he slurred, and Sabie knew he was going to buy more booze. She snapped the mandolin back into its case while he levered himself painfully up with his crutches.

"You're not taking care of yourself, Parker," she observed. "If Monika were here, she'd make you eat a proper meal."

Parker settled his semi-focussed eyes on her. "I'm taking care of what counts," he said, tapping his shirt where it covered his heart.

Sabie helped him hang his mandolin on his back so that his arms would be free for his crutches. "I'm setting up near the water," she said. "If you want to jam a little, later . . . ?"

"Maybe," Parker said amiably, shaking his head *no*. "Break a leg, Sabie," he said, which was his way of wishing her luck.

"Yeah, break a leg, Parker," she replied as the traffic stopped to let him cross the road.

Heading in the opposite direction, she dodged cars as she made her way to the open-air part of the market. She was in luck. There was an empty spot on the benches by the water. Security couldn't get her for playing there, she could just be practising her music while she watched the Aquabus go by. Kids could get away with more than grown-ups anyway.

"Play us a tune, duckie," said a man in a blue cap as she sat down.

"All right, I will," she promised, and grinned.

He put two fingers into his mouth and whistled. "Bea! Come and hear this!"

Bea turned out to be an old lady, not like Estelle, but fresh and crisp in a white suit, with a round straw hat and a straight back. Like a grandmotherly Lady Di, thought Sabie, warming up with one of her own compositions.

"Can you do 'When Irish Eyes are Smiling'?" asked the man, slipping an arm around Bea's waist.

"Sure," said Sabie, dipping into it. It was one of the pieces she and Monika had played on St. Patrick's Day.

"It's been so long since I've heard that," said Bea. "But it brings my old home to mind."

"Your old home!" exclaimed the man. "You were born in Idaho!"

Bea leaned her head against him. "But Father was from Ireland, you know. And a singer. Do you know, 'Dear Old Donegal'?"

Sabie shook her head. She liked the woman's voice, which had a soft lilt to it, and her warm eyes. To please the couple, she played "If You're Irish, Come Into the Parlour," and jazzed it up a bit. Bea took her companion's arm and they danced on the seawall, spinning round and round, sending pigeons and seagulls flying. After a minute, a couple of teenaged girls joined in, hopping around like Scottish Highland dancers. Pretty soon there was a crowd watching, parents with babies on their shoulders, kids licking ice cream cones, a couple of dogs chasing the pigeons whenever they cared to land.

"Thank you, duckie," said the man, wiping his red cheeks and brow with a hankie when Sabie had played all the Irish dance tunes she knew. "This is our first time out from Winnipeg. But you can be sure we'll be back, Bea and I. You're better than the sea air for what ails us."

When the man dropped a twenty into Sabie's sun hat, she was so surprised she nearly dropped her bow. "Thanks!" she called after the couple, then rolled the bill and stuck it into her sock.

After that, she leaned against a railing and played a mix of bluegrass standards and her own compositions. Lots of people put money into her hat. One lady gave her a bag of organic cherries, and a sticky toddler on a harness dropped a melting chocolate ice cream cone in among the coins when his parents were busy strapping on their bicycle helmets. "Oh, good one, Tyler," the boy's dad said, and fished out the cone apologetically.

As the sun slid closer to the bay, the tide came in with a salty breeze. Sabie loosened the hairs of her bow, laid the violin in its case, and slipped it back into her backpack. Then she took a quarter from her sun hat, wiped it off and found a pay phone.

"Thank you!" a mechanical voice said pleasantly, after Sabie had inserted the quarter. "You're welcome," she replied automatically, before she realized she was talking to a machine. She rolled her eyes as she tapped in Estelle's number.

Estelle did not answer. "Pick up the phone!"

Sabie called into the receiver. Then, after thirty-seven rings, she hung up and pocketed her quarter. Estelle was probably out in her front yard again, clipping dandelions with scissors — she hated to let the dandelions get the best of her.

Sabie hung up and headed down to Kits Beach, carrying an almost-too-ripe pineapple that a fruit stand lady had given her. It wasn't much of a walk, but by the time she got there a slight spattering of rain had begun, from a single fat cloud in the sky.

She lay in the sand anyway, her back against a log, enjoying the gritty smell the rain raised from the sand, and trying to keep her eye on the black speck that was a far-off swimmer. It was dumb to swim so far out, she thought. If that swimmer got caught by a boat's propeller, who would know? Who would ever know?

Something hit her in the stomach, hard. She sat up, surprised. It was a big multi-coloured beach ball.

"Sorry!" laughed a man, running over and scooping up the ball. He was wearing shorts and a red baseball cap.

"Shira, heads up!" the man called, spinning the ball on his fingertip, then tossing it backwards over his shoulder to a toddler in a matching cap who didn't even try to catch it. She just fell into the sand, giggling.

Sabie watched the two play. The child called the man Daddy but she didn't look like him. He was blond and curly-haired, she was dark and straight-haired, maybe Mexican. Was her mother dark, Sabie wondered, or was Shira adopted? Sabie imagined the man walking up and down long rows of cribs in an orphanage, looking for just the right baby. She saw him stopping in front of Shira's crib, spinning a ball on his finger, the baby laughing. "Heads up!" she imagined him saying, "She's the one!"

Where was her own father right now? Sabie wondered. She got to her feet, rubbing the crusty sand from her damp clothes. She felt chilled. The chubby drops of summer rain had soaked her, after all. The question returned. Where was Colin at this very moment, right now, while Shira was playing with her dad by the sea and Sabie was watching?

"Want to join in?" the man called, tossing the ball to her.

Sabie tossed the ball back, shaking her head. Still, after that she smiled as she watched them play. They weren't strangers any more, not really.

"Good going!" she cheered when Shira finally caught the ball in her chubby grasp.

When Shira grazed her knee and her father scooped her up and kissed away the sandy smudge of blood, something caught in Sabie's throat. She remembered how, during Monika's dancing with life lesson, she had fallen and skinned her own knee.

She would have given anything if she could close her eyes and remember that Monika had soothed the sting with a kiss, but Monika had hurried her to her feet, eager to continue the lesson. Sabie sighed. If Monika were beside her now, maybe she would wish the same thing too.

You can't change the past, not even the small things, and maybe not even the memories, Sabie whispered to a crow that passed between her and the emerging sun.

"Ready or not, here I come!" called Shira's father. Handicapped by the beach ball, which he carried between his calves, he chased after his giggling daughter.

Sabie couldn't help wondering: had Colin ever played with her that way? Maybe, when she was little. He and Monika had never been married, hadn't even lived together all that much, so she hadn't spent as much time with him as other children spent with their fathers. But there used to be pictures . . . she remembered pictures. One of Blue Karma in their pickup truck. They'd been travelling across Canada, getting gigs. Colin was in the cab; the rest were riding in the back like berry pickers, Sabie in a travel bed under the open sky. Another of her in a princess costume. Colin hadn't been in that photo, but Sabie could remember that he had given her the costume and come to take her out trick-or-treating. She hadn't wanted to be a princess, she'd wanted to be Batman, so she'd sulked. And then Monika, who always seemed to cry when Colin was around, had complained that Batman was too violent and princesses too sexist, and that Hallowe'en was all about white sugar and companies making money off of little kids, so Colin had gone home and Sabie hadn't gone out at all. "Let's not make a big deal out of this," Monika had said to Sabie, and switched off the porch light.

It was funny, the way Sabie could remember the pinch of the princess tiara on her head, the impatience in Monika's voice, but she couldn't remember even Colin's face. What had happened to those photos, when had Monika thrown them away?

"Bye-bye!" Shira called in her sweet baby voice as she and her father made their way back to the parking lot.

"Bye," Sabie echoed, watching them go. Then there was a kind of quiet, just the waves and the birds, no people-noises. The sun really came out, a low-in-the-sky, straight-in-your-eyes, after-dinner kind of sun. Gee, Estelle would like it here, Sabie thought. Maybe she wouldn't like the idea of catching a bus and getting down here, but she'd like it once she arrived. She could take off those pink socks and wiggle her knobby toes in the sand, eat hot french fries from the stand, watch gulls swoop down for crusts . . . . It would take her mind off Morty. And Candace. And her stupid grandchildren.

Sabie smashed the soft-skinned pineapple against the log, and sank her teeth, chin and cheeks into the sweet, pulpy flesh. Juice trickled down her chin, around her ear and onto her neck. It's a good thing I'm not sleeping in Chateau Chrysler anymore, she thought, or I'd be ant food.

Then she washed herself off as best she could by scooping up brown seaweedy water from the tongue-end of the waves; the salt stung her cheeks, but tasted good. She went barefoot into the water, feeling its heaviness as it swung around her legs, scouring her gently with silt, wood debris and kelp strands. Sand washed away under her heels and she settled deeper, toes up.

Monika had always brought her here to the edge of the bay to talk about things, and now Sabie knew why, though she'd never wondered about it before. If you stood like this, where the ocean met the earth, and could feel the whole power of their joining under your bare feet . . . if in one turn of your head you could see the sky tumble down the mountainsides and across the tops of buildings and spill itself into the glimmering bay . . . then you could feel as though you were at the start of everything. You could go in any direction, and it would be the right one.

You could dance here, if you were like Monika.

You could even choose not to dance, not to push against the tide, maybe live in a regular house with a lonely old lady, maybe even let the social workers find you and send you to school, and it would still be all right. Because the sky and the salt and the wind and the sand and the cold and the crying of the gulls would all be here, never changing.

Sabie rubbed her cheek against her T-shirt, then turned and walked back to her backpack. She dug her wet feet deep in the sand as she walked, and they became thickly covered, Frankenstein feet.

Then she picked up her things, tucked her sandals into her pack, and began her way home, enjoying the way the drying sand tickled her leg hairs, like 7-UP bubbles popping.

Estelle had been right to send her out. It had gotten the basement out of her. Settled something else down, too.

Now, if she could just find a way to bring Estelle down here with her.

Chapter Eleven

The grandchildren came in the middle of *Charade*, just as Audrey Hepburn was trying to decide whether Cary Grant was a good guy or a bad guy. They knocked at the front door and when Sabie opened the door they came in. So much for the nailed-shut windows.

"Who the heck are you?" Mark asked, then shoved past Sabie without waiting for an answer.

"Hey!" sputtered Sabie.

Estelle must have heard the commotion, for she emerged on hands and knees from the living room. She didn't wait to find out what Mark and Sheryl wanted, but immediately began beating the wall with her hand. "No! No!" she screeched. "I locked the doors! You can't come in!"

"We're just here for what's ours," replied Sheryl. "You don't have to wig out."

She turned to Sabie, almost apologetically.

"Will you just tell her that we want to take what's ours? We won't take anything else."

Sabie stood holding the door handle, unable to move or think of a thing to say. Her tongue felt as heavy as a granite chess piece.

"Nothing is yours!" Estelle shouted, squeezing the handle of the cane that she had dragged along with her. She tried to rise, but couldn't. Nobody moved to give her a hand. "You treated him like vermin! Such children! No calls, none! You broke his heart!"

Sabie looked to see if either of the grandchildren flinched or looked ashamed, but they didn't. Sheryl was staring over Sabie's shoulder at Morty's bedroom, which was now Sabie's. Mark sighed, scratching his armpit.

"Look, we wouldn't be here if you just worked it out like a grown-up," he said, matter-of-factly. "You should see how Mom is, she's seeing a therapist about all this, it costs a hundred bucks an hour — "

"A therapist! *Feh!*" retorted Estelle, spraying spit. "You can't cure snake-eyes with therapy! Better she should see an exorcist!"

Mark turned to Sabie. "See? See how she is? What can we do with her?"

"Maybe you could just leave," suggested Sabie, finally finding her voice.

Sheryl pulled her sweater closer around her, and hugged herself with her arms as if the house were chilly. "I only need to find one thing."

"What?" Sabie, who had inventoried everything

in the house, couldn't imagine what that one thing would be. A letter, maybe, from Morty, telling them how much he had loved them and that he had kept all this stuff for them in Estelle's basement?

"What's it to you?" Mark asked. "Who are you, a neighbour's kid?"

Sabie moved next to Estelle and bent to help the woman up. "I help out with the cleaning here. I might know where something is," she said, reluctant to help them but wanting to get rid of them quickly. Laughter came from the television.

"Bonds," Sheryl said. "Mom told us he bought them when we were born. They're here someplace. They're not in his safety-deposit box."

"Sheryl's going to U Vic this fall," Mark explained. "She needs them to pay her tuition. Mom doesn't have enough money."

"What? Not enough money?" Estelle snapped. "She's got Morty's house, she's got his car. She'd be a rich woman if she'd stayed with him, instead of kicking him out and driving his business into the ground."

"We're just going to look around," Mark said, exasperated.

Estelle put her cane across the hallway to stop him, but he pushed his way through.

Sabie followed them around the house, at a distance. "You want me to call the police?" she asked Estelle at one point, but the trembling woman simply shook her head. Sabie watched as Mark and Sheryl turned over drawers, leaving their contents where they fell. They looked everywhere, under mattresses, in the freezer, under the sink. They didn't comment on the bicycles and toys in the basement, didn't seem to wonder, even, at who they had been intended for.

"Kosher beef tongue!" Mark exclaimed, staring into the freezer. "Uck!"

"Did you see what's behind the freezer, Mark?" Sheryl whispered. "Rat poop!"

Mark shook his head. "I don't know whose kid you are," he said to Sabie. "But when you get home tonight, tell your folks that this old lady belongs in a home. She's completely crazy. Look at this stuff!"

"She's going to get some disease or something, living here," Sheryl said. "It's pathetic."

They didn't find the bonds, though they looked everywhere, even sticking a screwdriver into the floorboards to see if any were loose.

"Do you think he was lying about the bonds?" Sheryl asked her brother, wiping her palms on her jeans. "Or maybe he sold them."

Mark had a sour look on his smudged face. The two of them had moved just about every dusty box, mousetrap and stack of newspapers in the house.

"I guess we'll just have to sell some more of his stuff, then," he said. "The old lady's going to have a bird, but, shove it, if she'd just give us the stupid bonds!"

Mark pried the picnic bench off the basement door, and the two of them began carrying Morty's collection of garage-sale radios, the two ancient computers and cartons of assorted appliances out to the car.

Sabie didn't help them, but she didn't run upstairs to tell Estelle, either. Let them take what they want, she thought. Estelle will never know, and anyway, this basement is a firetrap.

She sat on the next-to-bottom stair, watching them, musing over how much they looked like Estelle. Both of them had Estelle's long nose and heavy cheeks, and when Sheryl stooped to lift something, her back had Estelle's giraffe-neck curve.

Sabie glared at them from her perch. If you'd take a good look in the mirror, you turds, she thought, you'd be really ashamed of yourselves. How could you steal from the person who gave you your nose?

"Is there an electrical outlet around here?" Mark asked Sabie. He was holding a dusty television in his arms. When she didn't answer, he plunked the TV on the freezer and plugged it into the freezer's outlet.

"Just like I thought," he said with irritation. "It doesn't work. I bet none of them do. Hey, Sheryl!" He called to his sister, who was gazing thoughtfully at a collection of Barbie dolls. "We'd better try all the TVs before we take them. We don't want to end up having to haul this stuff to the dump."

Mark tried the televisions, one after the other. "I know we must look like creeps," he said to Sabie, yanking a plug from the wall by its cord. "But my father left everything to us and Estelle won't let us have it. My mother wants to call the cops."

Sheryl wiped the screen of a black-and-white television with her sleeve. "It's really disgusting when things get so stupid."

No kidding, Sabie thought. Did they even know Estelle claimed she'd been supporting Morty for years?

Mark unplugged the last of the televisions. "Only three of them work," he said glumly. "Two are black-and-white, we won't get much for those. And there's a colour one that's in pretty good shape but somebody's spilled paint on it."

"I'm really tired, Mark," complained Sheryl. "Let's just go."

Mark cracked his knuckles. "You know what? Why don't we swap this TV for the one Estelle's watching? A bit of paint won't make any difference to her."

"Hey!" protested Sabie. "They're not the same! The upstairs one is in a cabinet. She keeps photos on top of it. She loves those photos."

"She can move them to a table or something," Mark said, giving her a "what's it to you?" glare.

Later, Sabie would wonder whether things would have turned out differently if Sheryl and Mark had just left then, instead of going upstairs for the television. If they hadn't disconnected Cary Grant in the middle of a gentlemanly wink and dumped the myriad of black-framed photos and the heirloom doily onto the dining room table. Maybe then Estelle wouldn't have had to hang onto the television cord in a futile tug-of-war, scrambling along behind them on her knees until she was forced to let go at the front porch stairs. She wouldn't have stayed there, crying and tugging at her hair while Sheryl yelled from the street, "He wasn't such a great father, you know!"

Something happened to Estelle then. Sabie didn't really notice at the time — it was, after all, not surprising that Estelle was angry, tearful, trembling, and confused after what had happened — but later, looking back, Sabie saw that things took a bad turn that night.

Sabie slept in the next morning. When she awoke, she found the house empty and too quiet — or rather, not quiet, but just television-less. She could hear the buzz-and-butt of flies in a window, the clank of dropping wood at a nearby construction site, and the conversational murmur of traffic on Cambie.

"Estelle?" she called, pattering from room to room, her bare feet dodging the bones of last night's raid: slumped stacks of papers, styrofoam meat trays, a cracked photo-frame. Mark had left the substitute television on a chair.

She found her in the back yard, near Chateau Chrysler, hunched over like a widow praying by a grave.

"Weeding?" Sabie asked, surprised. Estelle rarely came into the backyard. She had barely the strength to manage the front.

Estelle started and sank back onto her haunches. Squinting into the morning light, she peered at Sabie. One eyelid drooped. "Bring more salt," she said. Her arm, raised to shade her eyes, was trembling. "The line has to go right around."

Sabie knelt down so that Estelle wouldn't have to crane her neck. "What are you doing, Estelle?"

"Salt!" Reaching into her dress pocket, Estelle

drew out a fistful of something that Sabie soon saw was salt, and trickled it back and forth across the walkway. "Salt! It's in the hall. Oh, Christopher Columbus, do I have to do everything myself?"

"I'll get it, Estelle. Take it easy," Sabie replied. What was Estelle doing? she wondered. The old woman must have crawled down the front steps, then made her way around the side of the house, through the long grass to the driveway. Why?

There was, as Estelle had said, a bag of road salt in the front hall. Someone, Estelle or her grandchildren, had pulled it from the cupboard — along with everything else. There were mountains of old *Western Jewish Bulletins* and Safeway flyers tumbled about. Sabie found an empty ice cream bucket and filled it.

"Here," she said, setting it by Estelle.

"What took you so long?" groaned the old woman, reaching into the bucket. "If we don't get this done, that devil will get in." Grimacing, Estelle dragged herself a ways, dribbling salt as she went.

Sabie crouched beside her, the wheaty tops of the grass tickling her shoulders. She, too, made a line of salt.

"Like this?"

"Yes." Estelle's voice was indistinct, slurred almost, and Sabie glanced over to see if she'd forgotten to put her teeth in. But they were in. Maybe they had slipped out of place.

Sabie pressed the long grass flat so that she could kneel on it. Then she made a big show of sprinkling the salt.

"Not like that!" cried Estelle. "Do you think I have salt to spare? Make a line. A line!"

"Is this some kind of Jewish holiday thing?" Sabie asked. Estelle had told her about some holidays, one where nobody eats for a whole day, and another where people sleep in little leaf-topped huts in the backyard. Maybe this was a special summer holiday to remember when those people in the Bible, Sabie couldn't remember their names, were turned into pillars of salt. Sodom and Gomorrah or something.

"Holiday? *Feh!* The devil doesn't take holidays," Estelle muttered.

Carefully, Sabie trickled a line of salt around the yard. She moved much faster than Estelle and had done the front, sides and back before Estelle had finished the driveway.

"It's done," she said at last, clapping the salt off her hands.

"You didn't leave any spaces, did you?" Estelle asked.

"Nope," Sabie lied. Or maybe she wasn't lying, she reflected. How big a space did the devil need to get through?

"You go back to the house, then," said Estelle, sounding calmer. "I'll come."

"Let me help you," said Sabie, taking Estelle by the elbow. Estelle's scalp had turned pink from the sun, and her head was wobbling as if her neck was a spring. Why didn't she take off that sweater?

"No, no," crabbed Estelle, waving her off. "I'll get there myself. Leave me alone."

So Sabie moved from room to room, picking up the things that were scattered everywhere. By daylight the house looked ransacked. Drawers everywhere had been opened, some of them overturned. Pictures had been shoved aside. Sabie gathered up brittle pink negligees (had Estelle really worn these?) and enormous old brassieres that smelled of rubber, and stuffed them into drawers, trying not to mix them with the ties and greyed underwear that had obviously been Morty's (or maybe Estelle's husband's). Photos, knick-knacks and envelopes she tried to arrange neatly on the nearest surface. It was a bit like trying to clean up a trailer park after a hurricane, she thought; the lives of Estelle and Morty and their ten thousand distant but photographed relatives had been blown together, defying sorting.

Lifting a dim tintype of a couple with military bearing, Sabie began to wonder about her own grandparents. What had they been like? What did they look like? Monika hadn't liked her parents while they lived, and her feelings for them hadn't softened after they'd died. She'd never told Sabie why, and now Sabie would never know. Had they even known they had a grandchild?

Things were only slightly more in order an hour later, when Estelle crawled up the front porch and pulled the screen door open.

"See? She's trying to kill me, that devil Candace," Estelle said with a scowl when she needed Sabie's help to get back onto the sofa and out of her sweater. Her bare arms were like french fries, too thin for her body. Her bad arm hung limp.

"Maybe," Sabie admitted.

Estelle pulled a tissue from her sock and wiped her nose. Then she held out her foot. "There's something prickly in my sock," she complained. "A burr. Take it out for me."

"Let's get out of here and go to the beach," Sabie suggested, giving the sock only a cursory inspection. "We need a break."

Estelle ignored her. "I need another Kleenex. Reach it for me." Sabie passed her the tissue and Estelle tucked it into her sock. She slipped the dirty one into her brassiere. Sabie looked away.

"Tea would help." Estelle's voice was porridgey. She leaned back into the sofa cushions and closed her eyes. Sabie went to the kitchen and made tea, filling the kettle up in the utility room and bringing it to boil on the one element that still worked. Then she pried a bag from the pile of dried used tea bags that Estelle kept next to the stove, and made two cups of tea in jam jars.

In a funny way, she felt comfortable in Estelle's kitchen, like she was playing a game that she'd finally learned the rules for. She remembered how chaotic and filthy the kitchen had seemed that first day. Now, she knew the reason all Estelle's dishes were sitting on the counter, covering every bit of its surface: Estelle kept them there because the cupboards were too high for her to reach. The cereal and matzo cracker boxes stood out on the table for the same reason. The dirt was there only because Estelle couldn't see it.

"Did you remember the sugar?" Estelle asked, taking the tea, and Sabie just smiled. Estelle sipped the tea, her forehead unknotting in the steam.

"Oh, Christopher Columbus!" she said suddenly, sloshing tea onto her dress. "We haven't salted the drains! She'll come up the drains!"

"I'll do it," promised Sabie, humouring her. She obediently poured a handful of salt into various drains, both working and non-working. A little into the toilet, too, which did work, thankfully. Old ladies can sure be strange, she thought.

"I read somewhere that if you put salt on them, they shrivel up," murmured Estelle when Sabie returned. "Or was that slugs?"

"Well, maybe you should tell me where she lives and I'll take the salt over," Sabie replied, grinning. Estelle didn't return her smile, though, but closed her eyes and curled up on the sofa like a child.

Sabie, who felt heavy and tired and breakfastless, and still had the socky smell of drawers in her nostrils, slouched in the high-backed upholstered chair. It was early afternoon, but the day felt used and exhausted.

An arm of sun reached through a tear in the curtains and warmed Sabie's face. In a moment she was almost asleep, dreaming that she was cycling over a cool, rock-slapping creek. Monika was just ahead, moving swiftly, the guitar on her back reflecting the shadow-dance of the sun in the trees.

Estelle mumbled something, and just for a moment Sabie was pulled back to the day, heavily, like water winched up from a well.

"...it's too late now," Estelle was saying, "I've lived my whole life and now I know nobody will ever love me ... "

There was pain in Estelle's voice, and Sabie struggled to meet it. There was something she could say, something she should say . . . but she just couldn't quite find it. The sun's caress and the room's warm stuffiness filled her head with something thick and lulling, a memory of comfort, of being rocked to sleep by strong, musky-smelling, masculine arms that shut out the world of sharp words and bruising corners . . . . Whose words, whose arms? Sabie wondered, and then she was pedalling hard again, up an incline, pursuing Monika's familiar, far-away back.

Chapter Twelve

Estelle was weaker. Sabie could see it now. She had slipped down some internal hill, perhaps of age, and didn't seem to be able to make her way back up.

Estelle's bad arm was worse, almost useless. One leg began to tremble. An eye drooped, making her look perpetually half-asleep. She'd always been grouchy and sharp-tongued, but now she combined that with a kind of vagueness. She spent a lot of time gazing at things, the calendar for instance, or a spoon, for no apparent reason. It was as if something had popped in her brain and she saw things differently now, Sabie thought. But a change like that couldn't happen just because your TV was stolen, could it?

Was this what happened to all old people? They just woke up one morning and found that everything had changed?

Estelle made Sabie touch up the salt line several

times a day. People began to notice; a neighbour's nanny came across the street to ask what she was doing. "It's for slugs," Sabie explained. "It's a bad year for slugs." And Estelle began writing amulets to ward off evil.

The amulet-writing was more puzzling to Sabie than the salt line. The salt line reminded her of other people's superstitions, like throwing salt over a shoulder for good luck, or not walking under a ladder. But with the amulets, it was clear that Estelle was seeing something that Sabie did not see. They were always the same, written on Safeway and Home Hardware flyers and then left on the front porch. The words looked ordinary enough: peas, corn, milk, cereal, tea. To Sabie, they could have been shopping lists. Estelle, however, insisted they were the answer to a difficult problem rabbis had been working on for centuries.

"I'm not so dumb," Estelle beamed, tapping her head. "The rabbis will be around to pick the answer up, and then I'll be on 'Oprah'!" In the meantime, the wonderful answer, Estelle said, was powerful enough to burn the eyes of the devil, should she come snooping around.

"Don't step on those!" Estelle screeched one morning when a flyer carrier accidentally kicked one of the amulets, coming up the steps.

"Lady," the youth retorted, "someone's going to break their neck!"

"There's such a big pile of them now, Estelle," Sabie said gently, when the carrier had gone. "Can't we move some of them round back?"

"Oh, Christopher Columbus," groaned Estelle. "Don't you understand how important those are? Without them, they'll get me. They'll put me in the Louis Brier."

Sabie was not able to convince Estelle that nobody was coming, now that Mark and Sheryl had taken what they wanted. The daughter-in-law that Estelle so feared probably had no idea of the condition Estelle was in, and probably wouldn't care if she did.

In fact, if anybody phoned Social Services about Estelle, it would be Sabie. For Sabie was beginning to wonder. Every day, Estelle was becoming a little more mixed up. She wouldn't leave the hallway, except to go to the bathroom. She ate and even slept there, by the front door, her cane at her side. She never washed and, Sabie thought, she was beginning to smell a lot like Henry.

At first Sabie thought it was just the shock Mark and Sheryl had given her. Maybe, with some good food and a little time, Estelle would be her old, crabby self again. So she made a trip to Safeway for some parsnips, onions and potatoes, got a little of that gross-looking beef tongue out of the freezer, and made a palatable soup. Estelle enjoyed it. But she was as queer as ever afterward. "Thank you, Ginny," she said to Sabie.

One morning Sabie read an article about lonely Jewish seniors in an old copy of the *Bulletin* and dialled the number given in it.

"Jewish Family Services," was the crisp answer.

Sabie's hands were shaking. She almost put the phone down. "Um, I have a grandmother . . . . She's very old . . . "

The voice softened. "Did you want to order Kosher Meals on Wheels, dear? Or speak to a volunteer who could visit her?"

Sabie crouched low behind an empty box of cornflakes, even though she knew Estelle couldn't hear her from the hallway. "She's living by herself," Sabie whispered. "She can't really look after herself any more. Is there anybody I can talk to?"

"What's your name, dear?"

Sabie coughed. "I can't really give you my name. I . . . I don't want to let you know who my grandmother is yet. I'm not sure that I should be phoning."

"Fine," the woman said, to Sabie's surprise. She connected Sabie to another person, who passed her along to yet another. Finally, Sabie ended up speaking to an occupational therapist named Susan Landau.

"If you'll just give me your grandmother's name," said Susan, "I'll look her up in our database. She may already be receiving some kind of home care."

"She's not," said Sabie.

"Well, she probably is eligible. We may already have sent someone out to evaluate her. But the fact is, if someone doesn't want to let us into her house, we can't force her. Not as long as she's of sound mind."

Was Estelle of sound mind? "She sleeps on the

hallway floor," said Sabie slowly, "and she puts salt outside her house to keep the devil away. But she doesn't really seem crazy. She still plays chess."

The occupational therapist clucked her tongue. "This happens so often," she said sympathetically, "and most people aren't aware of it at all. When I worked for Social Services I had a client whose apartment was filled with boxes of tools. There was a path through them from his bed to the door, that's all. Mice lived in them."

"What happened to him?"

There was a sigh on the other end of the line. "He ended up in the hospital. He fell and broke his pelvis. But until that happened, there was nothing we could do. He just couldn't bear to be parted from his tools."

Sabie wondered whether the old man missed his tools in the hospital, if he knew that he would never see them again. She hoped that he'd been allowed to keep at least a boxful.

"She has to crawl to the bathroom," admitted Sabie, feeling like a traitor.

"Does she? Oh, dear. That's not unusual, though. It's probably safer than walking, if she's unsteady. Some people want to stay in their homes until they die, and I suppose that's their right. It's usually more upsetting for the family than for the senior."

Susan put her on hold for a moment to take another call, then returned to the line. "I'd be happy to come out and assess your grandmother. Depending on her needs, we could arrange for someone to visit her once a week, or place her in an adult day care program so that she would have some stimulating social contact. We could also ask the Health Department to send someone in to clean, do the shopping — "

"How much does that cost? She doesn't have much money."

"She probably wouldn't have to pay anything," Susan told her. "Where does she live? If she's not too far, perhaps I can come by this afternoon."

"I'll call you back," replied Sabie, and hung up.

"Estelle?" she called, padding down the hallway. Estelle sat up from her heap of quilts, blinking. Her hair was wild about her head, like fog. She never combed it any more.

Sabie squatted beside her. "Have you ever thought of having somebody come in to look after you?"

"You look after me," Estelle said, fumbling with her chin the way she sometimes did, as if she were adjusting her teeth.

"Somebody better than me," replied Sabie patiently. "A nurse or somebody. Jewish Family Services — "

"Them!" exclaimed Estelle angrily, struggling to her knees. "They've been trying to get their noses through my door for years!"

"But . . . "

Estelle grabbed onto the telephone table for support, nearly upending it. "They're in with that devil, of course. Once they're in here, they'll pack me off so fast . . . " She groaned, either from the pain of drawing herself up, or from the thought of the old folks' home.

Distraught, Estelle began fumbling in her pockets, looking, Sabie knew, for salt.

"It's okay, Estelle. I already salted."

"God sent you to me," Estelle said, smiling at her like a reassured child. Starting towards the bathroom, she paused and looked back at Sabie.

"God sent you," she repeated. "God I can trust, no one else. The whole world is trying to tell me how I should live. Have I ever told the world how it should live? All I want is to stay here."

That didn't sound so crazy.

Estelle was in the washroom a long time. Sabie made tea and hot instant oatmeal. She felt guilty for having made the phone call even though she hadn't mentioned Estelle's name.

Estelle was still in the bathroom when the letter carrier rang the bell.

"Hello?" said Sabie, opening the door.

The letter carrier handed her two bills and a sweepstakes entry form. Sabie looked at him curiously. He didn't leave, but just stood there.

"Yes?"

"I thought something might have happened to Mrs. Fogel," he said, shifting the weight of his bag. "All these piles of flyers . . . I thought perhaps she'd fallen."

"It does look strange," agreed Sabie. She searched for an explanation. "It's a recycling thing."

"Right," said the letter carrier, as if he understood. As if he could. But he didn't leave. "Who are you?"

"Oh," said Sabie, caught off guard. "I'm, uh,

Ginny's daughter. Ginny's daughter's daughter. You know, Estelle's niece, kind of."

He grinned. "Well, Estelle's kind of niece, I'm glad you're visiting the old lady. It's time someone did." Turning, he loped down the stairs three at a time and cut across the lawn. Halfway across the yard of the unoccupied house next door he turned and waved. Sabie waved back.

"Estelle? Are you okay?" Sabie called, turning in again.

There was a moment of silence, then Estelle called back. "Oh, Merry Krechtzmus! Bring me the cornstarch."

Not another weirdacy, Sabie thought, rummaging through the kitchen cupboards resignedly. She found the box after ten minutes of hunting (it was on the table with the cereal) and, opening the bathroom door just a little but keeping her head discreetly turned, sent it skidding across the floor.

"What's it for?"

"I've got the sour stomach," Estelle said. Her voice sounded weak.

"Well, tea's ready when you are," replied Sabie, having no idea what a sour stomach might be.

Estelle didn't come out and didn't come out. Sabie plugged in the small television that Mark had brought up from the basement and adjusted its colour. Then she played her violin. She thought of going out but decided to stay just to make sure Estelle was all right. Besides, she had to use the washroom, too.

Finally the bathroom door opened.

"You okay?" Sabie called, opening the front door. There was an awful smell coming up the hallway. Maybe she wouldn't use the washroom just yet.

Estelle was pushing the cornstarch down the hall. "Oh, I've got it bad," she said weakly, and Sabie saw that she was even paler than usual. "Make me some cornstarch milk. I just took some in water, but milk's better. My mother taught me that."

"I made you oatmeal, Estelle," replied Sabie, recoiling from the grimy box in the old woman's hand. "You should eat something. Anyway, if you're not feeling well, I'll get you something at the drugstore."

"*Feh.*" Estelle pushed the cornstarch onto the footstool, found her cane and pulled herself onto the sofa. "That stuff will kill you. Cornstarch in milk, there's nothing like it. My mother taught me that. It binds you up inside."

Sighing, Sabie grabbed the box of cornstarch and put it on the counter. It took her awhile to get it to mix in with the milk, but finally it did, more or less. She heard Estelle bang the bathroom door shut again. Darn! Sabie hadn't had a chance to use it yet.

"Estelle? I have your milk."

There was a silence. Then, "You're too late! What a mess! What took you so long?"

Standing there waiting, feeling foolishly unsure of what to do, the glass cold against her palms, Sabie suddenly thought she knew what it meant to grow old. She'd grown used to the way Estelle crawled about her house, not bothering with the cane. She'd grown used to her slight deafness, her shouts. But this was different. Being too old to make it to the bathroom on time was . . . awful. This was death coming like the devil Estelle so feared, crueller than the heartless daughter-in-law. Monika's death had been different, not stealing anything from Monika but time.

Was Estelle about to die?

The notion was so unexpected that Sabie almost dropped the milk. She set it on the hall table, sloshing a little onto the mail. Estelle had so often complained of being old, had so often spoken of dying, that somehow Sabie had assumed that Estelle had always been old and complaining. She must have known, yet she'd never thought that once Estelle had been her age and could run and walk.

Monika had talked about the dance of life. She'd meant grand things, like making a new world with her daughter, turning an overlooked corner into a home, funnelling good strong feelings into the strings of a guitar. But what about Estelle's end of life, when the dance became a dance of just getting to the bathroom on time? Did that dance have just as much meaning as Monika's?

Sabie brought Estelle clean clothes and a plastic bag for the soiled ones.

"Wash those, a little vinegar will get them clean," directed Estelle, clinging to the doorframe for support.

"Okay," promised Sabie, but she threw the bag in the garbage. "Goodbye, pink socks," she said, wrinkling her nose.

As she cleaned the bathroom with a pail of soapy water she remembered guiltily how often she had let Monika do the chores. Monika had never gotten angry about it though. Often Monika hadn't felt like cleaning up, either. Then they'd just let the stuff pile up until one of them felt motivated.

They used to have a chalkboard each, little ones. They'd write their problems on them and every evening they'd show each other their chalkboards and try to solve the problems together. It was one of Monika's home–schooling ideas. Sabie would usually write things like, "I want to be able to go places by myself," or "I need friends." Monika would scribble, "I want a great gig," or "I don't want to have to be the boss." Sometimes they would both write about an argument they were having; other times, they would be silly things, like "I want a Jeep," "I want to open for a Joni Mitchell concert," or "I want to buy the Museum of Anthropology and live there forever."

Monika always said that the one thing she didn't want to see on Sabie's board was, "I wish my mother would stop nagging me." Not that Sabie couldn't write that if she needed to. But Monika didn't want to be a nag. So instead of nagging, she tried pep talks. If that didn't work, she just let go — and the dishes didn't get done.

You couldn't simply let things slide in a situation like this, though, Sabie thought. Then she wondered, what would happen to Estelle if one day she just left, went chasing that life Monika had trained her for?

Estelle drank her cornstarch milk. Sabie couldn't watch. Somehow, drinking cornstarch seemed a lot like drinking Polyfilla.

She picked up her violin and then, reconsidering, opened Monika's guitar case and took out the guitar.

"So you can play that, too," commented Estelle, from the sofa.

"Mm," murmured Sabie noncommitally, plucking at the strings as she tuned the guitar. She hadn't touched the strings since just after Monika's death, although every night she slept with one leg thrown over the guitar in its quilted case.

Surprisingly, her fingers found the music right away. It was as if Monika were there with her. No, not with her — *in* her. When they'd played together, she had always followed, bending to Monika's selections, Monika's tempo. Now, the music came from her, and back to her; she saw by Estelle's face that the music was better than cornstarch.

The music filled the space between the young girl and the old woman, seemed to push the mustiness from the darkened room. It was Monika, Sabie thought wonderingly. The guitar was calling back part of her, bringing her strength back into the room. Sabie sang along a little, songs that she and Monika had written together, and hummed to others.

This was like dancing on the beach, freeing the heart and letting it run. Not the way Monika had shown her, with arms and feet, on sand and stones. Or with questions and answers. But with music. "Go with it, Estelle," Sabie whispered, her fingers strumming. "Dance with it. It's not over; it's not over . . ."

Estelle's good hand patted her lap in time with the beat. She even talked along with the music a little, not exactly singing, but putting something of herself into it.

"We're not bad together, Estelle," Sabie said between tunes. "Maybe we could get a gig at the Louis Brier."

Estelle's lids drooped over her milky eyes. "Did I tell you Morty's birthday is coming soon?" she murmured. "Morty liked a good tune."

Sabie watched the old woman draw a shabby pillow against her breast and clasp it there. She could read nothing in the tired, sagging face. Was this quiet moment in her own living room, away from the clutches of a nursing home, a victory for Estelle, or a meaningless bit of boredom to be passed over quickly?

Sabie recalled busking with Monika, the smell of fries and souvlaki, the mewling of gulls wheeling down for a bit of bread and music. She shifted restlessly.

"Well, then," she said finally. "How about a bit of Peter, Paul and Mary?" And even though she knew Estelle wouldn't know it, she began "Light One Candle." Just because of the smells and sounds of Monika it brought back.

Chapter Thirteen

Estelle's sour stomach eventually settled down, but by then she seemed to have shrivelled. Her eyes were sunken and filmy like those of a shrink-wrapped fish, and her skin chalked like plaster. Soon Sabie began to feel as if Estelle's mind had curled around one thing, Morty's birth date, then fixed there. Her constant preoccupation with the calendar reminded Sabie of a muddy wet blanket that she had once draped over a post to dry: lifting off the dried blanket, she had found that it rigidly kept the shape of the post and could not be smoothed.

Sabie fought these changes as best she could. She gave up on the small battles, like being called Ginny. It didn't really matter about that, she figured. Lots of old people get mixed up about names. She tried, instead, to fight the shrivelling of body and mind, to pull Estelle back to where she had been just the week before.

She cooked her things that were round and plump, like stewed end-of-summer apricots and steamed Christmas plum pudding (from a marked-down can). And tinned minestrone soup, with fatty chunks of lamb and slippery noodles. She put daubs of margarine in Estelle's consommé, so that little grease bubbles chased merrily around the rim of the cup. But Estelle wasn't interested in these things.

"Estelle, you can't do this, you have to eat," Sabie protested, when Estelle pushed away the consommé and reached for a cracker.

Estelle fidgeted with the calendar that she clutched perpetually these days, and said nothing. She had shrivelled so much that she couldn't use her false teeth for chewing any more. They would clack uselessly and then fall out.

When Sabie found that there was no way to reverse Estelle's physical shrivelling, she tried to retrieve the spark that had once been inside Estelle's mind.

"Tell me about how you rescued your cousin from Yugoslavia during the war," Sabie would say, because questions like that had once kept Estelle talking for hours. Sabie used to hate it when Estelle talked about her relatives, all just names now, all dead. Estelle didn't know how to tell a good story. She was more interested in where people sat on her family tree and how much they weighed when they were born than she was in good gossip. Sabie used to do anything to wriggle out of a relative story, even fall asleep. But now, she tried hard to coax one out of the old woman. "Tell me again, how many sons did your brother Harry have?" Nothing.

What Estelle did talk — or rather, mumble — to herself about, was Morty's birthday: August tenth, the ninth of Av in the Jewish calendar. Estelle seemed to think there was something magical in that day. Sabie learned, after much careful listening, why that day in particular seemed so important to Estelle. It was the day that Morty, weighing five pounds two ounces, had arrived unexpectedly soon, halfway between Estelle's house and her sister's store, on an Indian reservation in Saskatchewan. It was also the anniversary of his proposal to Candace. Sabie learned eventually from the Jewish calendar that the ninth of Av marked the anniversary of the day in ancient times when the Temple was destroyed and the Jewish people were forced to flee Israel and start new lives in unfamiliar places around the world. It was a day of mourning.

"I know that you're sad about Morty," Sabie said as gently as possible, "But maybe if you do something on his birthday it will make you feel better. We could plant a flower or make his favourite cake, maybe." But Estelle kept rubbing the smudged entry on the calendar with her finger and did not look up.

Sabie still went out to busk, but not often and not for long. Usually, when she got back, Estelle was right where she'd left her. By the door, on the floor, the calendar near her dirty pillow. When Sabie came in, Estelle would continue her one-way conversation just as if no time had passed. Sabie wondered whether Estelle even knew she had gone.

One afternoon, Sabie was out longer than usual.

She'd run into Parker on the island and they'd hung around together. He bought her some licorice-raspberry tea, which he swore would end the stomach pains she'd been having. The shadows were already lengthening when Sabie got home. A cold had settled into her chest, and she planned to go straight to bed. Her head was throbbing. Since Estelle had taken to propping a chair up against the front door, Sabie went in through the bathroom window.

Something was different. Sabie could feel it in the air. More than that, she could smell it. There was an acrid, smoky smell mingled with the familiar mildew-and-Henry odour.

"Estelle, did you leave the element on?" she called, teetering on the pile of junk in the tub as she pulled the window shut. No answer.

"Hey, Estelle?" Sabie pulled open the bathroom door.

An oily river of smoke flowed along the hallway ceiling.

"Estelle!" Sabie cried and raced to the kitchen. She'd known this would happen, Estelle would leave the heat on under something and fall asleep. Sabie was so sure that a pot was scorching on the burner that when she got to the kitchen and saw that everything was perfectly normal, except for the hovering cloud of smoke, she stood for a moment, frozen, her heart banging in her ears.

"Estelle!"

There was plenty of smoke, but it wasn't thick. If she bent over, she could make her way beneath it. Oh, why hadn't Estelle ever put in one of those cheap smoke detectors? Sabie wondered, hoping that Estelle wasn't lying dead somewhere.

She found Estelle in the living room. Not dead. Not even unconscious. The old lady was sitting on the floor in front of her overstuffed sofa, surrounded by a sea of paper, burning something in a metal wastebasket.

"What are you doing?" Sabie shouted. "Don't you know this house is a firetrap?"

Estelle pushed a wooden-framed photo into the fire, her knobby fingers seeming to pass right through the flames.

Sabie crawled toward Estelle, coughing. The photos gave off an oily kind of smoke that burned her lungs and eyes. It was probably poisonous.

The old woman's eyes were strange, still sunken, but glittering like metal beads. Her hands fluttered around the basket, batting at any sparks that floated free. Her mouth was working; she was intoning something that could have been an incantation. Because Estelle was looking at the fire it took Sabie a moment to realize that Estelle wasn't casting a spell but speaking to her.

"I've got to burn it all, burn it all," she was saying, her voice as thin as wind whistling under a door. "Take it all back to the beginning."

Seeing as the house wasn't immediately going to burn down, that the fire in the wastebasket was more like a barbecue than an inferno, Sabie squatted down beside the old woman.

"We should take this outside," she suggested. "Smoke can do funny stuff to your brain, can't it?"

She'd once listened to a firefighter speak about how breathing in smoke could make people do crazy things, like run back into a burning building or hide in a closet.

Estelle ignored her.

"Get that bit there," the old woman said, pointing to a corner of paper that was hanging over the rim of the basket. "Oh, Christopher Columbus," she groaned when Sabie hesitated, "Do I have to do everything?"

Sabie grabbed a porcelain figurine and used it to poke stuff back into the fire. The basket was glowing red.

"What's your plan, Estelle?" she asked, thinking that if she could figure out how Estelle's mind was working, she would be able to talk her into putting out the fire. "Is this some kind of new way to keep Candace out?"

"No, no no no no. Are you blind?" Estelle cried, passing her hand across the heaps of paper. "It's his birthday. My son's. Mine."

"Your birthday, too? Really?"

Estelle squinted at Sabie through the smoke. "Every mother's life begins when her child is born."

"I guess," Sabie agreed, pulling a box of papers toward the fire. What *was* all this stuff that the old woman was burning?

"For me, this day was a curse."

Sabie looked up, startled. "Having a baby was a curse?"

"Not the baby! The day! The day!" Estelle shouted, sounding almost like her old self. "The ninth of Av. It's a bad day for Jews. Morty wasn't supposed to be born then, he was supposed to be a New Year's baby, in September, on Rosh Hashanah. But I walked too far, I wanted to see my sister. So he came."

"But he was fine, Estelle. A healthy baby. A beautiful baby. You told me."

A golf trophy hit the pail with a clang. With a cry, Estelle snatched at her hair, tearing out some and throwing it into the fire.

"Estelle!" Sabie cried, grabbing Estelle's arms and pinning them to her sides. "What are you doing? You'll hurt yourself!"

The old woman didn't struggle. Instead, she whimpered. "I'll tell Mama, Ginny. It's my mistake, so I have to fix it."

Sabie let her go, settling back on her haunches. She didn't know what to do. She almost got up to call 9-1-1. Then she didn't. Estelle seemed really crazy this time. If they saw her like this, they'd take her away for sure.

What would happen to Sabie if Estelle was gone?

Estelle picked up a ribbon-tied packet, a bundle of Morty's report cards and a couple of class photos. She dropped them into the flames. Immediately the edges were blackened. EMILY CARR ELEMENTARY the top card said in two rows, then . . . ILY CARR MENTA . . . then the last bit of blue wisped away.

"What time is it?"

Sabie peered across the fire at Estelle.

The old woman's face was drawn up tight with some kind of fear. Through the rising smoke, she looked ghostly, as though her skin was going to slip off her bones and float away. Sabie felt that Estelle was preparing to leave this world, slipping out of her earthly body the way she might slip out of a nightgown.

"It's nine thirty, Estelle. At night. Tell me what you're doing. I want to help." Sabie touched Estelle's arm soothingly.

"No!" Estelle yelled, shoving Sabie's arm off. "No time for that. Don't you get it? He was born at ten. All this stuff has to be burned by then!" There were tears on Estelle's cheeks, the smoke making mud of them.

"It's okay," Sabie murmured, "I'm here to help you. We'll get it done."

Her words seemed to placate Estelle, who fed the fire wordlessly while Sabie tried to figure out what she was thinking.

This was Morty's birthday, Estelle had said. What did that have to do with burning all this stuff? Was it some kind of religious thing, that all of a dead person's stuff had to be burned on the day they were born?

Sabie watched Estelle. The woman's movements were convulsive, driven. Like someone being poked hard, Sabie thought. No, Estelle wasn't doing this out of religion.

"Estelle," she said, trying for an everyday voice, "tell me again. Is this something to do with Morty's kids? Are you making sure they won't get this stuff? Hey! Watch out!"

Estelle, in turning toward Sabie, had ignited a pile of papers with a flaming scrapbook. Sabie swatted out the fire with a sofa cushion.

"My sofa!" cried Estelle.

"Don't worry about the sofa," Sabie replied, wiping her nose on her wrist. "A little fire isn't going to be any worse for it than Henry was."

A wheezy kind of sound escaped Estelle, but no other protest. Sabie thought Estelle had forgotten the question about Morty's kids, but after a moment the old woman answered.

"Of course it's about them. There won't be any them. I'm starting over, don't you see? Starting over. If you start over, there's nothing, don't you know? My beautiful baby will have another chance. Not to be born on the ninth of Av."

Sabie was starting to feel dizzy. No, not dizzy. Sluggish. Or thick. Something like that. Like trying to walk underwater. She didn't know which way to turn her thoughts. The fire seemed to leap taller in the basket. Laughing, Sabie thought. It's laughing at us. "Better open a window," she told herself, but then couldn't remember why.

Around the fire, the room was growing darker. The fire seemed to be sucking night in.

"Wreck Beach," Sabie said, coughing a little between words. Her head buzzed, her thoughts swirled loosely like smoke rings. "Mom used to make me fires like this at Wreck Beach. We'd make stick toast."

"Merry Krechtzmus," muttered Estelle irritably. "What's that got to do with anything?"

"Hey, you sound like you did the first day," exclaimed Sabie, heartened. "Cranky." Her tongue felt thick, as if it had fallen asleep. What *was* that buzzing?

In her hand was the big baby picture of Morty that used to hang in the dining room. Looking at it, Sabie could feel the answer seeping into her, what Estelle meant by starting over.

"You're trying to erase Morty's life!" she burst out.

Estelle was crawling across the floor, scraping stuff towards the fire. "By ten, by ten, by ten," she said over and over.

The wastebasket was set exactly where Morty had died. Sabie remembered how Estelle had told her the paramedics had lain Morty down here, pushing on his chest to get his heart started.

"Yeah," she said, surprise giving her the energy to turn her heavy head and grin at Estelle. "You're not crazy after all! This makes sense!" She felt that she had swum through some kind of booming water cave, parting the water at its sun-dappled surface.

Sabie began to help Estelle, handing her things to feed the hungry fire. At some point, Sabie wasn't sure when, the fire left the metal basket and saved them the trouble of carrying stuff to it.

"His bedspread!" Estelle called, over the snapping and hissing, and Sabie knew exactly what she meant. Not bothering to duck the smoke, Sabie went to Morty's room and grabbed up his blanket and pillow, tripping over them as she carried them back to the fire that was now lapping along the old carpet. "Oh no you don't," she chided, stomping on those flames that nibbled too deeply into the carpet.

The dropped bedding made a still square of dark in the centre of the leaping light; then Estelle threw a stack of burning paper onto it. Sabie went back several times for Morty's clothes, passing each arm-load to his mother for arranging on the floor. Some-how, she felt, this burning-backwards fire was going to make everything all right for Estelle, burn back the ties between her and Morty until they were just stumps, ready to bud anew. Estelle wouldn't have to blame herself any more. It almost made Sabie cry, the joy of being able to do this for Estelle. Helping. Like in a family.

It was only when, dragging an old set of tennis rackets down the hall, she saw the fire consuming a black shape of Monika's that she woke up.

"No!" she screamed.

Staggering to her feet, she grabbed not the gui-tar case but the prostrate form of Estelle, and began dragging her to the door.

The fire was booming now, there was a wailing in her head that wouldn't stop. Flames shot up the ancient curtains, seeming not to burn them so much as lift them. They had to cross the fire to get to the door — how had it got around them like that? — but Estelle wouldn't budge.

"Me too, me too," Estelle was saying, but Sabie didn't know or care any more what she meant.

She pulled the protesting woman as far as she could, then, hunched and holding her hand over her face, ran to the door for air.

It seemed she just touched the knob, and the house exploded outward.

And the most unsurprising thing of all was that she exploded right into Morty's arms.

Chapter Fourteen

It wasn't really Morty, of course, but a firefighter who caught Sabie as she stumbled through the doorway. She was whisked off to the hospital, where she was weighed, fed and scrubbed until she shone. The next morning she was turned over to Social Services, which didn't surprise her one bit.

The social worker's name was Ann. Her ancient Honda Civic smelled like cigarette smoke and tuna. There were papers everywhere. She scooped some off the front seat and threw them into the back to make room for Sabie.

"I should have left you in that hospital, you know," said Ann, sliding into the driver's seat.

"I would have run," retorted Sabie, with a scowl.

Ann sighed. "Look," she said, "You're probably in shock. Whoever you are, you've been through the grinder. But give me a break, will you?

Already today I had to take a baby away from his parents, you don't want to know why, and give another baby back to two pyromaniacs even though the foster parents want to adopt him. On top of that — " Ann swung the Civic energetically around the corner, then slammed on the brakes to avoid hitting a dog. "Oh, blast," she said, "why do I bother?"

Sabie slid her eyes sideways, taking Ann in without letting her know. This was no social worker. This was what, the Terminator? An escaped lunatic? Despite the thorough washing she'd received at the hospital, Sabie's lungs still spasmed to clear themselves of the smoky remnants of Morty's burnt-up life. She coughed violently and wondered if there was a box of Kleenex somewhere in Ann's junk.

The Civic careened around corners like something from a cartoon cop chase. Papers, coffee mugs, mateless shoes, a briefcase, flew everywhere. Indifferently, Sabie noticed that Ann ran two red lights.

"Oh . . . Christmas!" barked Ann. Abruptly the Civic cut into a parking lot and came to a squealing stop between two vans.

"Out! Out! OUT!" screeched Ann. "You want them to catch us?"

The last words were uttered just before the door slammed. Bewildered, Sabie followed the disappearing social worker through the glass door of McDonald's.

"Two coffees, two cherry pies," Ann said to the boy at the cash, then turned to Sabie. "Not too quick on your feet, are you? Haven't you outrun a cop before?"

Sabie's jaw dropped.

"Didn't see that speed trap at the corner of 33rd?" Ann grinned. "Well, neither did I, till too late. Figured she was going to radio ahead to her partner, so thought I'd better pull in here. Don't think she could've caught my licence, do you?"

Sabie didn't say anything, just stared. All those times Monika had warned her against Social Services, saying how they would turn her into just another number — she'd never mentioned anything like this.

Ann looked at her tray. There were two large packets of fries on it. "No, no," she said to the earnest-faced clerk. "Not fries. Cherry pies." She added something in Chinese, and the boy grabbed up the fries and hurried away.

"ESL student," she explained to Sabie. "Started yesterday during my coffee break. This time, ten months, his English will be as good as mine. You'll see."

The clerk hurried back, pies in hand. The manager followed, hovering.

"Great employee," Ann said to the manager. "Great suggestive seller. Wouldn't have thought of those pies myself. Give him a raise."

She slid the tray off the counter and, with great, long strides, loped across the restaurant to a corner booth.

"Used to work for McDonald's myself," Ann explained, sliding a cherry pie packet over to Sabie.

"Back then, my English wasn't too good, either. Heck of a job. Everybody mumbles. Especially the ones with kids. But it got me through school. Taught me people skills too." Ann snorted and lit a cigarette.

There were napkins on the tray. Sabie wiped her nose on one.

"There," Ann said, exhaling. "Thank God. Think we made it, or they would've been in here by now. The cops, I mean. I can't afford another ticket. Got twelve points already and the rates just went up."

Sabie bit into the cherry pie. It burned her tongue. "Ow," she said.

"There's a warning on that packet," Ann said. "Or at least there used to be. CAUTION: CONTENTS HOT. Can you read?"

" 'Course I can read," Sabie snapped.

"Good," Ann replied. "Not everybody can, you know. Now, why don't you tell me about yourself."

"You can't buy me with a cherry pie."

"Wouldn't try to," said Ann, flicking her cigarette ash into her coffee lid. She pushed the lid over the NO SMOKING notice.

Sabie sipped her coffee, then added a packet of sugar. She slid forward on the bench so that her feet would touch the ground. She hated feeling short.

Ann snapped open her briefcase and pulled out a notebook. "Okay," she said. "Tell me everything. Begin at the beginning. Who are you? You're not the old lady's granddaughter."

Sabie didn't answer. Off in the corner, a kid

stood on a chair and pressed the wall button that started the merry-go-round. Monika used to do that, start it for her so she could ride it.

Ann tapped her pen onto the paper. "Look," she said, not unkindly, "If you think I'm trying to rush you, it's 'cause I am. I still have a teenager to move today. The fourth time in a month. And her boxes aren't getting any lighter, let me tell you. So if you feel like I'm rushing you, that's why. It's not personal."

"Well, if I don't answer, that's not personal either," retorted Sabie. She pushed her finger through the pie crust.

Ann put down her pen. "I know I sound pushy," she said. "But look at it this way. The cops could've taken you in. They think maybe you had something to do with the house burning down. But they let me have you. I promised them I'd at least find out your name."

"Bugs Bunny," answered Sabie. She bent to fold her socks down so that they wouldn't rub her singed legs.

Ann could have gotten mad, but she didn't. Instead she changed the subject.

"Cherry pie isn't exactly the meal one would expect after what you've been through," she said. "I was planning to take you for Chinese. But the speed trap, you know."

The pie was good though. Sabie hadn't realized she was hungry. She could feel the coffee starting to work too. Rhythmically, she kicked the table leg.

"Okay, I'll ask the questions, and you tell me

the answers," said Ann. "If you don't answer, I'll put that down. Somebody, though, is going to find out. I hope so, for your sake."

She sounded friendly. Sabie kind of liked her. But so what, she was still a social worker.

"Name? Do you want to try that again?"

When Sabie didn't answer, Ann scribbled in her book. "Bugs Bunny. Right. Age?"

Sabie took the last bite of pie and chewed noisily.

"Eleven to twelve," wrote Ann. "Are you a runaway?"

"Runaway from life," muttered Sabie.

"I'll put down yes," said Ann. "Look, I've met lots of runaways. I know what you've been through. Believe me, if — "

"I'm not a runaway. I'm an orphan," said Sabie.

"Orphan. Sure. Hundreds of orphans running around on the streets," said Ann. But she put it down anyway. Sabie liked that.

Ann leaned over the table. "I'm going to ask you this, but it's only to help you. Forgive me, okay?" She drew on her cigarette, then stubbed it out roughly. "You working the streets?"

"No."

"On drugs?"

"No."

"Got a pimp?"

Sabie twitched. "I'm not doing that. I told you."

"Where do you live?"

"Nowhere," said Sabie. Then, after a moment, "No, change that. Put, 'no fixed address'."

"A street kid? How long have you been homeless?" asked Ann, her voice sympathetic, not disbelieving.

"I dunno," said Sabie. "I'm not. I wasn't."

Ann rubbed her eyebrow. "I don't get this, Bugs Bunny. You're not a runaway, you're not working the streets, you say you're not homeless and you won't give me your real name. Or address. What's with this secrecy? Have you just robbed a liquor store?"

Sabie studied the wet brown ring at the bottom of her cup.

Ann looked at her thoughtfully. "Would you like a burger?"

Sabie didn't reply. Enough with the questions.

"Well, then, tell me why you were in the burning house, if Mrs. Fogel wasn't a relative."

"I'm the maid," said Sabie. That was sort of the truth.

Ann wrote that down.

"First maid I ever had to put in a group home," she said. "You don't fit any profile I have."

"Good," Sabie said with satisfaction.

"I have to take you somewhere now, Bugs Bunny," said the social worker. "It's a place where you'll sleep temporarily. It's dry at least. And I'll find you someplace better. If not your real home, then someplace. It'd help if you tell me your name, though. I don't have time to do a search. Really. If you only knew." She rose, scooped up their cups and emptied the tray into the trash. "Come on, we have to go."

Sabie followed her back through the glass doors.

"Don't think I don't care," said Ann. "I do. It's — Oh, NO!" Her voice rose to a screech. "They can't do that, can they?"

There was a ticket on the Civic, underneath the wiper.

"They can't get away with that!" cried Ann. "Whoever heard of giving a speeding ticket to a parked car? It's harrassment!"

She ripped the ticket off the windshield and peered at it. "Cripes, it's handicapped parking! Give me a break!"

A bunch of giggling four-year-olds carrying birthday presents streamed by the Civic, making for the door. Sabie melted in with them. She hadn't planned it; she just did it.

For Monika.

The smoke must have affected her brain, she thought, because it felt like everything was in slow motion. Even now, a whole day later. She passed through McDonald's, out the other door, and cut through the parking lot onto an alley, noticing all kinds of things — a smashed fry, a broken bike rack — but feeling nothing. Vaguely, she thought she should be scared, or excited, her heart pumping hard. Isn't that how you're supposed to feel when you run away from somebody?

Mostly, Sabie felt like she was still living in yesterday, that she would deal with today later. She should be with Estelle, not running from social workers. Where *was* Estelle? Where do they take old ladies in oxygen masks? There had to be at least five hospitals near Estelle's house. But maybe she hadn't gone to a hospital. Maybe she'd gone to an old folks' home.

The alley smelled of garbage and burgers. There was graffiti on the backs of some of the stores. *After the end of everything comes the reruns* was stencilled tidily over and over again on any bit of smooth surface. By an alley poet, Sabie thought. Here and there in screaming red spray paint were the boastful balloon letters of some gang insignia, and in a couple of places, right over the poet and the gang member, somebody had slopped on *DIE!* Dully, as if from a distance, Sabie noted the unfairness of it. There was plenty of wall for every wall writer, no need to obliterate somebody else's thoughts.

There was a chill in the air. It was getting past shorts weather. Coughing, Sabie left the alley and walked down a sunnier street. Even in the sun, though, she felt cold. She looked at the houses with their neat lawns and sparkling windows. Maybe a door would open and someone would call, "Sabie! Lunchtime!" like in that soup commercial, and she'd just walk in and sit down.

People left babies on doorsteps. Why not teens?

She coughed again, a cough that bent her double. It had really settled in her chest, that cold. She hadn't had a cold this bad since she was little.

She wished she could call Parker. She wished he wasn't a drunk. She wished he had a place and could take her in; at the very least, she wished he could tell her what to do. But he couldn't even save himself.

Suddenly, it was all too much. She couldn't pretend any more. She had nowhere to go. She couldn't busk; the fire had taken care of that. No violin. She didn't even have a clean pair of socks. And she missed Estelle desperately.

Whatever plan Monika had had for her, it wasn't going to work.

There was only one thing left to do. She sat down on the foundation forms for a new house and cried. The crying came from so deep that it dug up her cough, and in between sobs she coughed until she thought she would be sick from the straining. She didn't care who saw her.

Lots of things ran through her mind, pushing the smoky fog out and letting pain in instead. The roaring of the fire. How Estelle had screamed when Sabie had dragged her, the awful popping sound that Estelle's arm made when Sabie pulled on it. Knowing that Monika's guitar must have burned in the fire. Monika in her bed, waiting for coffee, dead. The heat in her own scorched legs. Monika on the beach, crying out at her to dance with life.

With a shuddering intake of breath, she stopped crying. Her face felt taut, puffy, like she'd probably popped every blood vessel she had.

When the car pulled up in front of her, Sabie wasn't surprised. She walked back across the bull-dozer-scraped earth, blinking when the sun glinted off the side mirror, and pulled open the passenger door.

"Hi, Bugs," Ann said, not even sounding angry at having spent almost two hours looking for her.

"Sabie," murmured Sabie, brushing her hair back from her face. She felt very still inside, like part of her was listening, she didn't know for what.

"Sabina Pincher. I'm thirteen."

Chapter Fifteen

The emergency shelter wasn't so bad. It would have been okay, if she hadn't been so worried about Estelle. Sabie had her own bed and meals were served by friendly people, an old guy with a ponytail and a young woman with a pierced lip. They gave her some hand-me-down jeans and a straw hat.

Sabie kept pretty much to herself. It wasn't that she didn't want to talk, but that she didn't know how to chit-chat. The pierced-lip lady kept asking names and offering Sabie cough syrup for her cold. The place was filled with people, kids, caregivers, social workers popping in and out. Everybody acted like they knew each other, but they didn't.

"My group home got shot out last night," said one girl over a spoonful of Manna cereal. "Some girl's ex drove by and put four bullets through the windows. Phoned in a bomb threat. They brought all of us here for the night." She went back to her chewing, not seeming to mind Sabie's silence.

At ten Ann picked Sabie up.

"I hate my office, so how about coffee?" She gunned the car along Broadway. "It's not an office, just a pile of junk behind a plant. No privacy."

"Hmm," Sabie murmured, staring out the window as she wiped her nose. If she fixed her eyes in a certain way, all the stores went by in a blur. Like coloured streamers. She hadn't spent much time in a moving car.

The coffee shop was a dark pit. Monika would never have taken her there. Not one vegetarian thing on the menu.

"They don't bother you about smoking here," Ann said guiltily. "And they're cheap." She had a habit of rubbing her cigarette with her thumbnail.

"Coffee," Ann told the waitress.

"Me, too," Sabie said.

"You're too young for coffee," Ann tsked as the waitress swished away.

"You ordered me some yesterday," Sabie pointed out.

"I did?" Ann seemed genuinely surprised. "I don't seem to have my head screwed on these days. Must be my workload."

"How's Estelle?" Sabie asked, getting to the point.

Ann rocked her hand in a gesture that meant, *so-so*. "I'll keep you posted," she said sympathetically. Sabie decided not to press her just yet.

"Sorry about running from you." She made the edge of the sugar bottle go *bump bump* against the arborite tabletop.

"Forget it," Ann replied. "I'm always losing people. One of my clients turned up in Portland, Oregon. With a baby, no less."

Sabie wondered about that. Should Ann be telling her all this stuff about other people? Wasn't it supposed to be confidential? But in a strange way, it made Sabie trust her more.

When the coffee came, Ann poured a stream of sugar into hers, then sipped it without stirring. "We have a lot of ground to cover this morning," she said. "Good thing they serve a bottomless cup here." The waitress brought them a copy of the *Province* but Ann shook her head *no thanks*.

"How do you feel about your father?" Ann asked.

"What do you mean?" Sabie returned. What was Ann up to?

Ann shrugged. "Has he ever, you know, hurt you? Done anything to make you afraid of him?"

Sabie mulled this over. Did Other Woman count for hurt? Did not knowing anything about him count for hurt?

"Why?" she stalled.

"If you slouch any lower, you're going to land on my feet," Ann said, smiling. "There's nothing to worry about. I'm just trying to help you, that's all. We've been in contact with your father. He lives in Calgary — "

"So I've heard," said Sabie bitterly.

Ann gazed at her thoughtfully. Her words were gentle, not pushy. "He says he wants you to come live with him. How would you feel about that?"

Sabie stared out the window. The café was on Granville Street, one of Monika and Sabie's old haunts. Parker busked in front of that liquor store sometimes. She craned her neck. Maybe he was there right now.

"Look," said Ann, "I'm not forcing you to do anything. I just want to run over your options, find out where you're at and maybe where you're going. There are other places too, you know, besides your father's. Foster family. Group home. You're probably too young for independent living."

"Yeah, right."

Ann leaned back against the vinyl bench. "Open up a bit, Sabie. Let me in. I've got about one hour to find out your whole life, set you on the right road."

Sabie lifted the heavy cup and dropped a napkin into the puddle of coffee beneath it. The stain was sucked along its fibers like dye into arteries. Like a cancer treatment. She raised her eyes. "Tell me what the autopsy said. About Monika. They must have done one." To Sabie's shame, it was Monika's Colin voice that came out of her.

Ann's cup was halfway to her lips; she set it down. "Your mom had cancer," she said gently. "Did you know?"

"Yes," whispered Sabie, feeling herself turn into a small child, and fighting it. "But it wasn't that bad. I only went out for coffee . . . I wouldn't have gone if it was time . . . " Tears came into her eyes then, stupid tears, tears that made a choking feeling at the back of her throat and spilled over her eyelids, even though she didn't want to cry, even though she stared out at a bus that had pulled up to the stop and with great concentration counted the people getting on and off. Three off; eight on.

Ann's hand closed over hers. "It's okay to cry. They know me here. Everyone I bring either cries or yells at me."

Sabie smiled through her tears. She accepted the tissue that Ann, with her cigarette-wielding hand, had fished from a pocket and passed to her. She was surprised there were no cigarette burns on Ann's jacket.

"The cancer helped us find out who your mom was," Ann continued gently. "We found her medical records." She squeezed Sabie's hand. "But it wasn't the cancer that killed her."

"It wasn't?" Sabie stared at Ann, startled.

Ann shook her head. "She had an aneurism. One of the arteries in her brain had a defect that made it weak. Probably she was born with the defect but never knew it. It was like a time bomb. When it ruptured, she died right away. There was nothing you could have done to save her, nothing a doctor could have done, probably. It wasn't because you went for coffee."

Sabie pulled her hand from Ann's and scrunched up the wet napkin. Some of the soaked-up coffee dribbled back into the saucer. The waitress refilled their cups.

Sabie remembered a lot of things about the day that Monika died, strange things. Such as the gnawed-on and still wet root of licorice that Sabie found on the bed next to her. Monika always chewed on licorice when she had gas pains or a headache that needed easing. Had she felt a warning pain before the aneurism, and reached for the licorice? Maybe there was something in licorice that weakens blood vessels? There had been a towel on the bed, folded around Monika's hairbrush and a sliver of soap. She'd been planning a shower, it seemed. People didn't plan to take a shower just when they were about to die, did they? So Monika mustn't have known, couldn't have been hiding it from Sabie.

There was a dull ache behind Sabie's eyes, and she held the hot coffee cup against her temple to soothe it.

"They're not hereditary, aneurisms," Ann assured her, reaching for the sugar bottle. "You won't — "

"I wasn't thinking that."

"She wasn't an alcoholic, or a drug addict either," Ann continued. "The autopsy showed — "

"Why would they check that?" Sabie was outraged. "Why would they think that?"

There was a flutter in the soft fold above Ann's left eyelid, and she rubbed it with her wrist. Ash fell from her cigarette. Parker was a much tidier smoker, Sabie thought, unreasonably irritated. Outside, a drunk stumbled against the window and slid to the ground.

"Ann, what happened to Estelle? Where is she?"

Ann exhaled a double stream of smoke from her nostrils, dragonlike, and gave Sabie an appraising look. "I'm not supposed to tell you," she said. "After all, it was a suspicious fire. We don't know for sure that you didn't try to bump her off — "

"Bump her off?"

Ann grinned. "Yeah. Bump her off. Rub her out. Snuff out her lights. I sound like a late-show detective, don't I?"

Sabie looked under the table. "I know I have a knife stashed in my sock somewhere," she intoned.

Motioning to the waitress for a refill, Ann chuckled. "Yeah, well, what I think is that the old lady's cheese slipped off her cracker. She did herself in. You're the hero who tried to rescue her, am I right?"

Sabie spun the salt shaker like a top and watched it wobble across the table.

Ann caught it and shook her head. "Aren't you going to tell me anything? What am I supposed to put in my report?" When Sabie continued her silence, the social worker shrugged. "All right. Here goes. I never could deny Bugs Bunny anything. Estelle Fogel is in Vancouver Hospital."

Sabie's throat was tight. She was hardly able to ask the question. "Is she going to be all right?"

"I don't know, Sabie."

"I want to stay with her," Sabie said, all kinds of feelings bunching up inside of her so tightly she could never let them out with just words. "I don't want to go to Colin's. I don't even know him. I want to stay with Estelle. She needs me."

Ann butted out her cigarette in the dirty ashtray, pushed her cup aside and leaned across the table.

142

"Sabie," she said, gently but firmly, "if I were your fairy godmother, I'd wave my wand and let you and Estelle live a beautiful life together. But I'm not your fairy godmother. I can make things happen for you, but real things. Not fantasies. *If* that old lady lives, she's going to be in an old folks' home. If she's lucky. But you — " Ann grabbed Sabie's wrist and shook it. "Look at these hands, how young they are, how you chew your nails! — you're just a kid, no matter what you think. You're not going to spend your life looking after paranoid little old ladies!"

Dropping Sabie's hand, Ann took another breath and continued with the same intensity. "Somehow, I don't know how, you've managed to stay out of serious trouble. I want to keep you out of it. You can't stay with Estelle. I think you should at least meet your father. But if you won't, then there're other options. Like I said, foster families. Just don't disappear on me. Your magic carpet won't stay afloat forever. Either you grab at something and give yourself a chance, or I'll be finding you in the morgue one day, needle tracks in your arm."

Ann spoke so forcefully that Sabie at first thought she was angry. But looking at her, Sabie was surprised to see tears in Ann's eyes.

"Hey," she protested.

"Hey."

Another bus pulled up to the stop, a blue suburban bus, and five smartly dressed shoppers got on. Just as it pulled away, a young mother with a stroller ran up and knocked on the rear window. The bus stopped, she picked up her baby, folded up the stroller, and boarded. Sabie could see the woman counting out her change as the bus moved into traffic.

"So, you think I should live with Colin, have a swimming pool, go to school in a Mercedes, eat pink grapefruit from a silver bowl for breakfast, and get my butler to take the Dalmatians for a walk, huh?" Sabie pushed her finger into the artificial sweetener packet she'd opened, then licked off the white powder.

"Hey, let's have a reality check here," Ann said. "Your father's not rich. He's an accountant for a transmission-repair shop."

"But Other Woman —"

"Margaux's not rich, either," said Ann, looking bewildered. She fixed her dark eyes on Sabie. "Margaux is a part-time librarian with multiple sclerosis. They have a four-month-old son, Dylan. Dylan Baez Guthrie Wharton. I couldn't forget a name like that. All my folk heroes in one little Pampers." The waitress dropped the cheque on the table and Ann slid it under her saucer. Then she wiped her nose on a napkin. "What is this, anyway, some kind of weird prejudice against rich people?"

Sabie's head spun. She'd had too much coffee; now her fingers were beginning to tremble. "But Monika said — she said they had a mansion. That Colin went after Other Woman's money." Why else would he have married Other Woman but not Monika? And why would Monika have told her that, if it wasn't true?

Pulling the cheque from under the saucer, Ann folded it back and forth, pressing it with her fingers until it had become a fan. Then she opened it up and smoothed out the creases. "I don't know what your mother told you," she said carefully. "I don't know what your family history is. All I know is that when I talked with Colin on the phone, he seemed like a nice guy."

"You spoke to him?" Sabie's stomach cramped. How many years had it been since she'd heard her father's voice? Vaguely, she remembered him singing by her bed at night, Bob Dylan and Joan Baez songs.

"He called. I answered," Ann said simply. "He's not a Martian on Spaceship Neuron that you need a NASA gadget to speak to. He's just an ordinary guy, with a big worry about his daughter. The way he tells it, he's been fighting for custody of you for years. He says Monika took you into hiding to keep you away from him. That mesh with what you know?"

"She said Colin didn't want me. She said Social Services would take me away from her if they found out she had cancer," Sabie mumbled miserably, rubbing the cold, soggy napkin between her fingers until it came apart.

"Bull!" exclaimed Ann, slapping the table with her open hand. "I hate that! I hate it when parents fight like that! Look at the mess it leaves!" She shook her head angrily, pushing three loonies over to the waitress.

Someone switched on the music system and

Celine Dion crooned across the diner. Sabie counted the diamonds that zig-zagged across the patterned carpet. She wasn't feeling well. Maybe she had to throw up.

"He-y-y," Ann said. "Things will get better. I promise you. I'll take you back to the shelter now. How about I set up a meeting with Colin on Friday? Just Colin and you, and me to help things along? How about having another go at family life, Sabie?"

Sabie rose, peeling her sweaty legs off the sticky vinyl.

"Thanks," she said, "But I don't think I want another go at family life. Not with my family, anyway. I think maybe I'll try one of those foster families you told me about. It can't be any worse."

Pulling her car keys from her bag, Ann gave Sabie an affectionate squeeze. "You're not so dumb, kiddo. You're not so dumb."

Chapter Sixteen

Ann told Sabie it would take a day or two to find a suitable foster family and that she might as well make herself at home where she was.

Making herself at home, for Sabie, meant wandering. There was a TV set at the emergency shelter, and a ping-pong table, but Sabie couldn't manage hanging about with a bunch of kids she didn't know. She wasn't good at that sort of thing. That became obvious right away.

"Do you think my hair's too frizzed?" asked a girl with the curliest hair Sabie had ever seen. "Deano did it for me."

"Yes," Sabie answered truthfully. "Not only that, it's longer on one side than the other."

The girl snatched a sweater up and left the room in a hurry. The next time Sabie encountered her, her hair was pinched back by barrettes and she was glaring at Sabie.

A few more exchanges like that, and Sabie concluded there were a few problems with Monika's policy about being upfront when asked for an opinion. So she grabbed the sweater Ann had given her and left. She couldn't wait any longer, anyway.

Her feet took her straight to Vancouver Hospital, a rambling grouping of old and new buildings. It was impossible to tell which building was Estelle's, but Sabie finally found an information desk to help her.

"She's not receiving visitors," the clerk told her, calling up Estelle's name on his computer screen.

"I just want to send a card up," Sabie lied.

But stepping off the elevator, she encountered a nursing station she couldn't avoid.

"Visiting hours aren't until two, honey," said a motherly looking nurse.

"I'm looking for my grandmother," Sabie said. "We were in a fire together and I can't wait another second to see how she is." She showed the nurse the healing burns on the backs of her legs.

"Well," the nurse softened. "I guess I didn't see you standing here, then, did I?" She gave Sabie a conspiratorial wink and bent back to her work.

Estelle looked awful. It wasn't just the bandages or that there was an IV feeding into the back of her hand. Her teeth weren't in, either, so her mouth was crumpled over her chin like a popped paper bag; but Sabie was used to seeing her like that. It was Estelle's skin: loose, dry and tissue-paper white. She reminded Sabie of the brown-flecked bodies of moths she used to blow off Estelle's window ledge. It seemed to Sabie that one gust from an open window would carry Estelle away, too.

Tentatively she touched Estelle's hand. Under her finger, loose skin slid across hard bones. She drew her hand back, thought again, and grasped the old woman's hand firmly. Estelle let out a long, shivering sigh and moved her head, exposing the singed side of her hair.

"You're wrong about there being a God, you know," Sabie murmured. "Because God wouldn't let old people get so stiff and wrinkly. It's mean."

She waited for Estelle to argue with her, wished desperately that she would, but Estelle lay silent.

"Oh, Christopher Columbus, do I have to argue with myself now?" Sabie teased, sadly. "Aren't you going to say, 'But the blueberry bushes get all stiff and wrinkly too, and do you hear them blaming God?' "

There were three other beds in Estelle's room, all occupied. Sabie kept her back to the others, pretending that she and Estelle were alone. It was easy to pretend. All the others, like Estelle, were elderly, frail white wisps under sheets. They probably couldn't even hear her. What was it about this hospital? Sabie wondered. Did people arrive here old and still like that, or did they shrivel up the longer they stayed?

"Estelle," she said clearly. Loudly, close to Estelle's ear to cut through whatever medication Estelle was on. "Estelle, it's me, Sabie. Ginny."

Estelle's eyes unsealed themselves a little.

Sabie stared into the milky discs, smelling the smoke that still clung to her hair. "Estelle, get well. Now. We've got to go home." The thin lids slid closed, slowly, slowly, and then they were stuck.

Estelle was dying. Sabie knew it. This was what dying was supposed to be like, she thought. Not the way Monika went, just like that. Estelle was slipping away, pulling away from her skin, leaving everything. Now that she'd unravelled Morty's life, she was unravelling her own. Sabie could read the determination in Estelle's upper lip. She was working hard at it.

Sabie bent over her. "Are you sure, Estelle? Are you sure there isn't more?" She wanted to say, "Like me?" but she held back. She remembered that Monika had tried to teach her about letting go, had told her that the living couldn't selfishly set obstacles in the path of the dying. "When it's time, it's time," Monika had said. Now, for the first time, Sabie thought she knew what that meant.

Estelle's white mouth whiskers flickered with each breath. The rest of her was as still as a barnacle.

The kindly nurse came in, checked Estelle's temperature by holding something against her ear, gave Sabic a wink, and left.

"You're going to fool that nurse, aren't you?" Sabie said. The nurse's chipper crispness had upset things somehow, and now Sabie felt like crying. She pulled a couple of tissues from the tiny bedside box and blew her nose. Things were churning inside her. She felt like her chest was being squeezed, but it may have just been the mugginess of the room.

There was just one thing to say. "Maybe I don't want you to go, Estelle," she murmured, wadding up the tissue. "Did you ever think of that?"

Sabie came back day after day. Ann knew, and let her. She couldn't find Sabie a foster family, anyway. Nobody wanted a runaway.

Day after day, Sabie watched Estelle shrivelling. She was continuing the shrivelling that she'd done before the fire, but more peacefully. She didn't go on and on now about birthdays. About beautiful babies, she-devils, and how everyone was against her. She just breathed. But each breath seemed to take a little more of her away.

Day after day, Sabie held Estelle's hand, watching the fluttering whiskers, admiring the delicate, dry creases that criss-crossed liver spots. The oldness of Estelle was, she suddenly realized, beautiful. But she hated that Estelle was shrinking away in silence. Not long ago — when? last month? — Estelle would grumble and bang her cane. You couldn't help but know what was on her mind then.

Sabie herself felt almost like she was dying. Her cold had spread. She felt feverish and wheezy. She had a recurring pain in her belly, she couldn't quite say where. She wanted to lie down and sleep. But she wouldn't leave Estelle.

One afternoon Ann brought something over to the hospital. It was Monika's guitar. Monika's hand-quilted case had burned, of course, and the guitar had been damaged. But Ann had had it repaired and restrung, and had found a good sturdy case for it at a pawn shop.

"Thanks," Sabie croaked, moved, unable to say more. Ann left her cradling the guitar and smelling the smoky, good wood smell of it. There was a nice ache in her.

When she tuned it, an orderly poked his head in and looked at her, but left without saying anything. Sabie let her fingers find the melody, pulling notes from the feeling in the air, from herself, from Estelle's empty face. After the melody came, the words came, too. Simple words, nothing special. Just things about Estelle.

> *She was sitting on her lawn, cutting the dandelions out.*
> *She was pulling the bad from the earth.*
> *Along came her grandkids, said get lost old potato bag,*
> *Took everything she had, and then some.*
> *Everything she had, and then some.*
>
> *She said, old witch, I know you're behind this somehow,*
> *She said, first my son and then his little ones.*
> *Evil Eye, you aren't getting more now,*
> *I've salted a magic spell, and then some*
> *Salted some magic, and then some.*
>
> *Well, she burned her whole life backwards in one night,*
> *Went back to her mama's lap, to the very start*
> *She said Evil Eye, I'm laughing at you now*
> *Burned a hole in the universe, oh, a hole now,*
> *Burned a hole, and I'm going in first.*

Estelle died while Sabie was playing. Sabie didn't know exactly when her friend slid away, what she'd heard of the song. She just noticed, about four in the afternoon, that the whiskers had stopped flicking. When she lifted Estelle's hand, the hard, knobby, bent-fingered hand, all the weight of life had gone. There was still dirt under the grooved nails, though, and Sabie supposed Estelle would be buried that way, with yard dirt under her nails and dandelion blotches on her fingers. It was something to take with her, anyway.

"I love you, Estelle," Sabie said, gently kissing the stained fingers. They didn't smell like Estelle's fingers. They didn't smell of Henry, of musty carpet, salted drains, Morty's fire or dandelions. They already smelled of soap.

Chapter Seventeen

There was a small park across from the hospital, no more than a patch of green grass atop a parkade, bisected by a smooth concrete path. Sabie found a bit of concrete that still caught the sun and lay down on it, soaking up its warmth. She should have been hungry since she hadn't eaten since breakfast, but she wasn't. Not really. She had a need to cling to something solid and warm and to lie still. Her head throbbed dully, but she ignored it by listening to the sounds of birds and traffic and people walking by.

"Do you think she's all right?" she heard a woman say, and someone else answered something that Sabie couldn't make out. She lay still, eyes closed, mouth slack, as if she were sleeping. She felt their eyes on her, but didn't care enough to open hers. They were just part of the background. The only thing important now was the concrete, its gritty warmth. After awhile, they went away.

Then she really did fall asleep, for when she awoke it was dark. Streetlights gave off a gassy yellow light into the park. She was cold and stiff. Her knees and the points of her hip bones were sore.

There was no point in going back to the shelter. She'd missed curfew and, anyway, she didn't want to talk to anybody. She was too cold to spend the night on a bench that was wet with late-summer dew. Estelle's place, and Estelle, were gone.

"Dance with life," Monika had said. Sabie looked across the road, at the hospital's empty parking lot, and across it to the busy lights of the city. The park was a small, still and empty spot amidst the traffic and wailing sirens, and that was the way she felt, too. Small, still and forgotten. Part of her knew that if she was ever going to live the way Monika had taught her, the time was now; she had to find her own strength and her own shelter. The other part didn't care, just wanted a warm place to lie down.

For a moment Sabie wondered whether she might be able to climb into Estelle's bed. Maybe they didn't know yet, about Estelle's dying, and she was still there. Or maybe they'd taken Estelle away but her bed was still empty. Then she smiled a little at her childishness. But she picked up her stuff, made her way across the road, in through the un-locked Emergency entrance and down a quiet hall-way to a restroom. It was a big, old restroom made in the days when people really rested. There were two rooms, the first with a broken-in sofa, two chairs and a long mirror. But anyone could open the door and find her. She went into the second room, the room with a sink and two cubicles. It was a pretty, uncared-for room, with ancient stained sinks and a gap-toothed mosaic on the floor. She took a drink and washed her hands and face at the sink, and then, looking around for something to do, wetted a piece of paper towel and dabbed at the grit on her knees. Finally she took her stuff into a cubicle, slid the bolt on the door, balanced herself on the lidless seat and stared at the hexagon floor tiles until the white ones began to leap out at her.

Sometime later, when the hospital had gone to sleep and only an occasional set of footsteps could be heard, Sabie left the cubicle and curled up on the sofa. It was soft in the middle. When she lay on her side, her ribs coiled together; she could hear them sawing wheezily as she breathed. When she lay on her back, her feet got cold hanging over the armrest. There was a pane of frosted glass on the door, and through it Sabie could see the grey shadows of hospital life. She wondered if that was the way everything had looked to Estelle's old eyes, a frosted-glass world.

Where was Estelle now? Sabie knew that the old woman's body was in the morgue, probably washed and waiting for somebody to do something with it. There was maybe even somebody Jewish watching over it; Estelle had told her that there was a group of volunteers that sat with the bodies of Jewish dead people until they were buried. But what about her soul? Had Estelle believed in an afterlife? Or, when she decided to die, was she accepting that it was all ending, that nobody would remember her, not even the grandchildren who had hated her without ever really knowing her?

What had Estelle said, that she'd grown so old and had never been loved . . . ? Sabie twisted on the too-short sofa. A lump made it impossible to make herself comfortable. It wasn't a broken spring in the sofa, but something in herself, in her stomach just below her heart. It was like something inside was all tangled up, throbbing angrily. She tried to remember where her appendix was; did she have appendicitis? No, she didn't think that was it. It was more like she had been hit in the gut. Like a bleeding bruise.

Closing her eyes, she pretended that Monika was with her. And then it wasn't pretending. She had called Mom, and she came. They were lying together, Monika's arm around Sabie's shoulder, supporting her head when she coughed. Mom was warm, safe . . . all the knobby bits of sofa became knobby bits of Monika. "My stomach hurts," Sabie whispered, folding her arms over it. "It's pulsing, Mom, see? Like a heartbeat." She felt Monika's hand rest on her stomach. "Shh, shh, it's all right. Go with it, go with it . . . . " The pain eased, and Sabie fell asleep.

Hours later, she jerked awake. Her ankle whacked a scroll of wood on the armrest, and she grabbed it to keep from crying out. "Mom!" she said, but her eyes were open and she could see that Monika wasn't there. Monika was dead. Monika was dead and she, Sabie, was supposed to be dancing with life and running from the system, running, running, not holding her ankle and pretending that a decaying sofa was her mother.

The pain in her gut was back, too, and now Sabie knew what it was. It was a fist inside her, squeezing, squeezing. It was Colin, pulling her to Calgary. It was Monika, setting Sabie on her own two feet with a push in the opposite direction, screaming at her to not give up now. "My little girl, my little girl," the knot throbbed, and then, "Don't go to Calgary! Don't go to Calgary!" For no reason at all, Sabie kicked the sofa.

In the hallway, someone was pushing something on wheels and thumping doors open. Sabie locked herself in a cubicle and used the toilet. By concentrating on the morning hospital sounds, she made the throbbing disappear. After awhile she flushed and went to wash at the sink. It had the sort of handle that turned off if you let go of it, so she couldn't use both the hot and cold water at the same time. Or wash her hair. She settled for washing her face. In the mirror, her face looked flushed, her eyes bright. Like she'd had too much sun, instead of a night in the ladies' restroom.

"You're an early bird," said a woman, pushing the door open and wheeling in a mop bucket.

"Visiting my grandma." Sabie lied instinctively. The woman gave her a thoughtful glance, then lifted the garbage bag out of the can, tied it, and set it out in the hall. Re-entering, she lifted a folded bag from the bottom of the can and hung it over the sides. Her body seemed too round to bend over that far.

"Where are your parents, hon?" she asked, filling the soap dispenser.

A wave of heat passed through Sabie, like she had just swallowed a mouthful of hot chili. She broke out in sweat, but didn't know why. The mop lady paused with a bundle of paper towels in her arms.

"Something wrong, hon?" Her voice was kind. She was just curious, that was all, and trying to be helpful. Sabie could have run out the door and she probably wouldn't have called after her. But Sabie didn't want to run out the door. She had no place to run to.

"Estelle died," Sabie said, beginning to shiver uncontrollably. Her teeth almost nipped her tongue, her jaw was going that fast. How could she be hot and cold at the same time?

"Was Estelle your grandma?" the woman asked, putting the towels back onto the cart, and taking a seat on the edge of the sofa.

"Uh-hunh," shivered Sabie, nodding her head up and down. Estelle was her grandma, in any way that mattered. The nodding made her head ache, and she stopped.

"Here, hon," said the woman. She opened her arms, and Sabie fell into them, curling her knees up on the sofa, holding onto the chubby neck with all her might, shivering and sobbing and saying things that couldn't possibly make any sense. And the cleaning lady held her and rocked her, and didn't even complain about Sabie's nose making her uniform wet.

In the end, of course, she ended up at Emergency, which was just around the corner and down the hall. Lillian (that was the cleaning woman's name) stayed with her until the police left and Ann came. Before she left, she took Sabie's thin hand in her plump one, and said, "Hon, when you're done crying and you're looking for something to smile over again, remember that you gave Estelle a very special gift."

Sabie sniffed, and Lillian pulled a tissue for her from a bedside box. "I didn't give her anything," Sabie said dully. Ann was standing at the foot of the bed. Sabie supposed she was there to take her back to the emergency shelter.

"Yes you did, hon. You gave her your love. Hundreds of old folks die in this hospital, but you're the first young person I ever found grieving in that restroom. That's something." Then Lillian gave Sabie a generous kiss on the cheek and left.

A nurse came and took Sabie's temperature. It was about the twelfth time somebody had taken her temperature or blood pressure. This nurse was a guy with a Mickey Mouse pin on his pocket and a nametag that said "Jamil, born to heal."

"You feel hot?" Jamil asked. "Your temp is pretty high."

Sabie shook her head irritably. "I'm freezing to death and they won't give me any blankets," she complained. "And I just want to get out of here."

"You're in luck," Jamil said, giving her a dazzling grin. "I'm a magician, and blankets are my specialty." Spinning on his heel three times and then uttering some magical gibberish, he thrust his hand through the yellow curtains and brought back a thin cotton blanket.

"You're going to get your other wish, too, I think," said Jamil. "We're probably sending you to Children's Hospital."

"But I'm not sick," protested Sabie.

Jamil waggled his eyebrows. "My guess is that you've got pneumonia, ascariasis, and maybe a touch of iron-deficiency anemia."

"What's that?"

Jamil put on his stethoscope and listened to Sabie's heart. "A bad chest cold, worms, and you haven't been eating very well, either. But don't tell the doctor I said so."

Ann moved to Sabie's side. "Is that serious?" She sounded concerned, not angry. Sabie twisted her head around to see her.

Jamil straightened. "They'll run more tests at Children's. I think she'll be just fine in a couple of days, though, as long as she doesn't sleep in parks or washrooms anymore." He rubbed Sabie's head as if she were a tired five-year-old. "Get some rest, short stuff, and don't run off any more. Give yourself a chance."

He left, and Ann sat down beside her. The visitor's seat was low, and Sabie looked down at her through the shiny bedside bars.

"I'm fine," Sabie said.

Ann sighed. "You're fine, but *I'm* having a heart attack. First you disappear from Waverley, then I get a call from Emerg saying that they have you on a stretcher."

"It's only because Lillian made me come," said Sabie. "That's what cleaning ladies do when they find kids in the bathroom."

Ann shook her head. She didn't say anything, just leaned her head back against the wall. Her shoulder was wedged against the sink, Sabie saw. She looked exhausted. Well, it was her job. Sabie hadn't asked Ann to come worrying after her.

"So?" Sabie broke the silence, finally. It wasn't like Ann to be so quiet.

Ann opened her eyes. The usual gleam wasn't in them. "One of my clients died last night," she said. "Heroin overdose. She was only fifteen."

Sabie pulled the blanket up to her chin and tucked it over her shoulders. She just couldn't seem to stop shivering. Fifteen. Not much older than Sabie.

"A street kid?" she asked.

Ann hesitated. "A runaway."

"What was her name?" Sabie couldn't help asking, she didn't know why.

Ann smiled gently. "When she was picked up for shoplifting, she said she was Donald Duck. Seems to be a lot of cartoon characters running around. But her name was Daphne. She was smart. I thought she had a chance."

"You need a cigarette," Sabie said. Sabie knew that look: tired, haggard, like she needed something to hold onto.

Ann thumbed towards a no-smoking sign. "But I do have something," she said, rifling through her overstuffed bag. Bits of paper, lottery tickets, and a thin paperback fell onto the floor. Sabie coughed into another small square of hospital tissue and waited. Finally, Ann drew out a plastic-wrapped chocolate cigar tied with a pink ribbon.

"One of the case workers had a girl last week," Ann said, breaking the cigar in two. She passed half to Sabie. "It's Purdy's, my favourite. Try it, you'll like it." She said the last part like a mad scientist, rolling her words exaggeratedly and hunching her shoulders around her ears.

They both popped the chocolate into their mouths at the same time. Ann chewed noisily. Sabie sucked hers, letting the dark sweetness coat her tongue and glide down her throat. It was good. The shivering stopped. She looked at Ann. The social worker's eyes were closed again. She looked discouraged. Or beaten.

"Eh, what's up, Doc?" Sabie quipped, trying to cheer Ann up. But it had a different effect.

The social worker opened her eyes and snapped forward on her chair.

"I'm not going to let this happen," she said, her voice tight. "I'm not going to let you run off again. Do you know what happens to cartoon characters on the street? Do you? Because if you don't, let me take you down to the morgue — "

"Hey!" protested Sabie.

Ann snatched a tissue from the bedside box and wiped her eyes. "I'm sorry. I shouldn't have said that. But — " she smacked the guardrail with her palm " — it's what I feel."

"What do you want *me* to do?" Sabie plucked at the blanket.

Ann sighed. There was a smudge of chocolate on the corner of her lip. "I've found a foster family that would like to have you. They're nice people, older, with grown kids. I know them well. I think you'd like them. And they live near a school that I think would suit you. But . . . " Ann took a deep breath and continued gravely, "When the hospital called me, I called your father. He's on his way here, without Margaux."

"What!" Sabie screeched. She felt betrayed. She sat up, swinging her bare feet through the guardrail and over the edge of the bed. A wave of nausea passed over her.

"Hold your horses," the social worker said, but not sternly. "He's going to take a taxi to my office when his plane lands. I'm going to fill him in on what's been happening to you. Then he's going to stay at the Holiday Inn — "

"The Holiday Inn!" scoffed Sabie. "Just the place to stay when you're visiting relatives you don't like."

Ann shook her head. "Why don't you give him a chance, Sabie? Just a chance. Monika got to tell you her side of the story. Now, let Colin tell his."

Sabie bent double, overcome by a fit of coughing that threatened to pull her stomach muscles apart. Ann leapt up and put an arm around Sabie, holding her tightly.

"Should I call a doctor?" she asked, sounding alarmed.

Sabie shook her head. "I'm going to chuck, that's all," she said. But she didn't. In a few minutes the coughing and nausea passed, leaving her with a throbbing headache. Ann wrapped the gold cotton blanket around her, tucking it around her feet.

"Chucking's not going to get you out of this one," Ann said, smiling gently. "If you don't want to live with him, you don't have to. But you do have to meet him."

"No." Sabie shuddered violently. Her teeth began chattering again. She clung to the cold metal guardrail.

"But why?" Ann stroked Sabie's hair. Sabie could smell old cigarette on her hands. She didn't want the stroking to stop. She didn't want there to be any more questions. Everyone always asked too much. Even Monika.

"Did Colin hurt you? Did he — "

"No!" Sabie leaned her head on the guardrail, feeling it press against her forehead, cold, then warming with her fever.

Ann didn't say anything, and after a moment, when the rail became the exact temperature of Sabie's head and there was nothing more to focus on, Sabie answered. "Because if Colin isn't who Monika said he was, then *she* wasn't who I thought she was."

When Ann didn't respond, Sabie continued, keeping her eyes focussed on the speckled linoleum floor. "Mom told me Colin didn't want me. She taught me to look after myself, so that Social Services —"

"That's me," put in Ann.

"Yeah," said Sabie. "So that you wouldn't get me and put me in a home. So I wouldn't become a cog in the system." She moved her head over a bit, onto a cool spot. She could see the scuffed toes of Ann's shoes.

"But if Colin wanted me, then . . . " Her voice shook, and she had to swallow to clear her throat. "Then, who was Monika? And why didn't she take the cancer treatment?"

"Sometimes parents hate each other," Ann said softly. "It makes them do crazy things. Out of spite. Or jealousy."

Sabie shook her head. It was more than that. It wasn't just that she was afraid of finding out that Monika had been jealous. It was all that Monika had taught her: about being honest about her feelings, about dancing with life, facing all that comes, being open to others. Monika had been the most alive person Sabie had ever known. Filled with something special, the thing that makes nuns want to become nuns, and mountain climbers want to become mountain climbers. It was like the sun was channelling through her, just because she had found a way not to close that off. But if she had lied about Colin, then everything else was a lie, too. What she'd said about dancing with life. About keeping Sabie out of school because schools would kill her love for learning. About talking being the best way to solve problems. About Monika loving Sabie more than life, even, which was why she didn't mind living in dumps so that they could hide from The System. One of her parents was a liar. But which one?

This time, Sabie did throw up.

Chapter Eighteen

Sabie liked Children's Hospital. There were playrooms with toys she was far too old for, but which she'd never played with as a child. There were even outside playgrounds on every level. You could zoom down a slide and pretend that you were sliding all the way down Oak Street to Granville Island. On Sabie's second day there, a writer named Sue Ann Alderson came to read stories and gave Sabie one of her books. It was *The Not Impossible Summer*, the book Sabie had started so many months ago.

"It has a happy ending," the author told her with a wink. "They're the best kind."

"It's good to see you curled up with a story," commented Ann during one of her visits. "But your problems aren't going to solve themselves while you read about other people. There's somebody waiting very anxiously at the Holiday Inn."

Sabie peered over the top of her book. "Why

doesn't he just go back to Margaux?"

Ann sighed. "He doesn't have to wait, you know. I told him he can come in here any time, that you're as stubborn as a . . . as a . . . "

"As a what?"

The social worker shook her head. "I can't think of anything as stubborn as you." She set a stem of grapes by Sabie's bed. "Anyway, he said he wasn't going to push. It has to be your decision, he said. But he gave me this." She fumbled in her bag and pulled out a battered envelope.

"What is it?" Sabie knew it was a stupid question. She was stalling.

"Oh, go on," said Ann, "It won't survive another day in my bag." She saw the look on Sabie's face. "All right, I'll go. I'm due for a cup of coffee anyway."

When Ann had disappeared through the swinging door Sabie ripped open the envelope and pulled out a selection of newspaper clippings, some of them years old. All of them were about Colin and how he was looking for his daughter. There was even one from this summer, "Come Home, Dad Pleads," which was all about how Colin had heard that Sabie was working the streets as a prostitute, and how he begged her to come home and start again. There were ads, too, from many newspapers, all beginning, "Persons knowing the whereabouts of . . . "

Tucked in with the clippings was a photo. It was of Colin, holding a chubby baby in his arms. He was standing in a doorway, leaning against a poster of Blue Karma. All the band members were in the poster, Monika and Colin too, but Colin wasn't looking at the poster. He was gazing into his baby's eyes, and he was smiling.

Sabie looked at the photo a long time. Then she turned it over. On the back was an ink footprint, and under it was "Sabina, 5 months." Across the top, in black felt pen, were scrawled the words, "I love you, Sabina. Please come home."

Sabie held the photo all afternoon. Supper was brought in and then carried out untouched. From her bed, she watched the sun set below Oak Street. Babies went to sleep. The hall lights were dimmed. Parents and nurses spoke in whispers. All the while, Sabie was holding the photo, not always looking at it, but just holding it, as if some secret knowledge that it held was going to flow into her.

And she thought. She remembered Monika, smiling, sagey-smelling Monika. Monika brewing peppermint and lemon balm sun tea on Jericho beach. Monika massaging a child's palsied limbs, and an old woman's arthritic hands, gently and knowledgeably, easing their pain. Monika meditating on Galiano Mountain, waiting for the sun to rise. Monika crying as she told Sabie that Daddy didn't want to see his little girl any more . . .

What was it Parker had once told her? That Colin was never cut out to be a musician. That he was a nine-to-five-jobber and a white-picket-fence kind of guy? Monika wouldn't have been able to live with that, Sabie knew. She was too full of dreams, of hopes for a perfect, meaningful world. Was that all it had been then, her life with Monika,

169

an endless running from a father who loved her but couldn't be who Monika wanted him to be?

If Sabie went with Colin, it would be like admitting Monika was bad, maybe even evil, wouldn't it? That Monika had done everything, even thrown away her own life, to keep Colin and Sabie apart. A person like that, there couldn't be anything good about her, could there? She was just like Candace, Estelle's devil daughter-in-law, turning a child against her father.

About two in the morning, a crib was wheeled into Sabie's room. There was a toddler in it, with casts on both arms.

"What happened to the baby?" Sabie asked the nurse who hovered by the crib.

"They just brought him up from ICU. They're overflowing down there."

"Yeah, but what happened to him? Did he get hit by a truck?" Sabie had never seen so much cast on such a small person.

The nurse stroked the toddler's cheek. "Shh, shh," she soothed him, even though he seemed to be sleeping. She looked over at Sabie. "He was pushed off a countertop," she said, angrily. "It's a miracle he doesn't have brain damage. He suffered a concussion."

"Pushed?" echoed Sabie. "Who would do a thing like that?"

The nurse shook her head. "His teenaged mother, I was told. Said she couldn't take it any more, the little guy just kept climbing up and turning on the stove."

"Is he going to be okay?" Sabie asked, her voice barely a whisper.

The nurse sighed. "I guess. His bones will heal. But . . . " She rubbed her cheek on her shoulder. "And to think I've been trying for a baby for eight years . . . " Her voice trailed off.

Sabie looked at Colin looking at her baby self. The photo was soft with sweat. Why had he gone to Calgary?

"Why are people so mean to each other?" Sabie asked aloud.

"I don't know, dear, I don't know," the nurse said, sighing. She dimmed the light over the toddler's bed. On her way out of the room she paused in the doorway and said, "You want to know something funny? The nurses in ICU told me that this kid's mother came to see him this morning, with a social worker. The mother brought him a car he can't even hold any more, and sat by his bed and cried. Hard to figure, huh?"

Sabie thought of Estelle. Of how she had died feeling that nobody loved her, that her life was a waste, all because Morty's children and their mother hated her. Seemed like Morty had struggled with her too. Maybe Estelle had brought some of it on herself, telling Candace she wasn't good enough to marry her son. But was that enough reason for Candace to teach Mark and Sheryl to steal from Estelle? For Estelle to feel that her life had been cursed?

The toddler gave a little cry, then went back to sleep. They'd probably given him something to keep him that way, thought Sabie. Nobody could sleep all plastered up like that. And when he woke up, he would have a lifetime of trying to make peace with his mother.

Monika was never going to get a chance to sit by her bed and cry like this kid's mother, Sabie realized, wondering whether Monika would ever have come to feel any remorse, if she'd lived. Maybe when Colin left her years ago, Monika had begun to see the world from a crooked angle and had never been able to get things straight again.

And that's when Sabie knew, although she couldn't have said how understanding came to her. She knew that Monika loved her, just as Estelle had loved Morty. And even though Sabie might never truly understand why Monika had done the terrible thing that she had done — whether it was just that she had loved Sabie so much she didn't want to share her, or that she really did in her heart believe Colin's way of life was wrong for Sabie and that they would be better off on the streets, or even that she had just wanted to hurt Colin — Sabie knew that she couldn't spend the rest of her life hating her mother.

As confused as she was about everything, Sabie knew that she loved her mother, and, even if in her whole life she never figured Monika out, Sabie wasn't going to waste time poisoning that love. She, Sabie, wasn't going to draw salt circles around herself to keep out every person who had ever done anything that hurt her. Pretty soon, everybody would be outside the circle. She didn't want to take a chance on ending up like Estelle, alone. Or like Candace, plotting.

Sabie pulled open her nightstand drawer and fished out the paper-wrapped quarter Ann had put there. She smoothed the paper over her knee, studying the phone number written on it, rolling the quarter over and over in her damp palm.

"If you're watching me now, Mom, you'll understand," whispered Sabie, sliding off the bed.

Then she squeezed the quarter tightly and padded barefoot across her room and along the smooth linoleum-floored hallway to the phone booth.

Epilogue

A Chinook swept through Calgary at the end of March, melting the snow and exposing the chickadee-down brown of the rolling foothills. Sabie, the sun hot on her sleeveless arms, stood barefoot at the thawing edge of the Glenbow Reservoir, savouring the slushy, squishy, Slurpee fridgidness of it as long as she could before she had to leap, ankle bones aching, to a stone.

"You're going to catch your death!" Margaux, keeping to the trail because of the stroller, called out a warning from high up on the reservoir's bank. But she obviously didn't expect any quick compliance, for she plucked Dylan from the stroller and sat down on the bank to nurse.

Sabie, squatting flat-footed on the stone, squinted out across the flat speckled whiteness of the reservoir. With the hills bare of snow, she thought, and the air so hot and dry, you'd almost think you were looking out across a giant salt-lick, or some sloughy mining pond. It was the biggest body of water in Calgary, but it was nothing like the beaches of Vancouver, wave-pounded and wade-able year-round.

Sabie had spent a lot of time with Monika on those beaches, working arithmetic problems in the sand with bits of driftwood, following the hoppings of a sand flea to see how much distance it could travel in fifteen minutes. Would Monika have been able to survive here, with Calgary's dry, dry winds, walled roads and cruel winters, if she'd got round to bringing Sabie back to Colin?

"Over here!" Margaux shouted, and Sabie looked up to see Colin, farther along the bank, a pack of groceries on his back, jogging towards them.

It hadn't been so bad here, Sabie thought, toss-ing a pebble into the slush. The pebble splatted, leaving an edge of brown around a disappearing hole. Margaux wasn't Monika; she was a small, bony, painfully shy woman who walked with a cane, not at all given to discussing things like the purpose of life or questions of ethics. But she'd taken Sabie to the library and got her a card of her own, and spent days finding just the right school for her, a flexible school that even Monika might have approved of, given the circumstances.

Dylan was fat and fast and into everything, but the best thing about him was the way he would fall asleep on Sabie's shoulder, his fat baby cheek tucked trustingly into the curve of her neck.

Colin was quiet, rarely moved to speak. He had calloused, wide hands and readable golden eyes; he liked using the pottery wheel at the community centre, eating french fries with mustard and carrying Dylan on his shoulders; but what he thought about Monika, the past, Blue Karma or politics, he never said. Sometimes, though, Sabie would find him lost in thought, one shoulder resting against a wall, shirtsleeves rolled up over his wristwatch, and if she made a small noise she could almost see the ghosts of the past leave his eyes as he greeted her.

The first time Sabie woke in the night and heard Colin, with his guitar, crooning to his croupy son, she had a sudden, lost memory of Colin singing by her own crib as she burned with fever. She lay, face pressed into her bunched pillow, breathing in her own hot breath, listening to the yearning in his rich, raspy tenor. Then she went to find him. He was sitting cross-legged by Dylan's night light. Dylan whimpered and she lifted him out of his crib, rocking on her heels with him as she joined Colin in the song she somehow remembered, "There are storms out on the ocean, there is calm beneath the sea, life's one long rolling current, child, roll along with me." How many times had those words, that voice, come to her like a ghost in the night?

At the end of the song, when Dylan's eyes had closed again, Colin pressed his hand against the strings of his guitar to shush them, and said to her, "Can I build you a room?" Meaning, will you stay? A few weeks later, he walled in a corner of the basement that had two windows and helped her to paint the new room yellow — her choice. When one day she'd helped wipe yellow paint from his hair, she'd known for sure that she was finished with being Robinson Crusoe.

They lived in a small bungalow, nothing at all like the mansion that Sabie had pictured, which was good in a way but also too bad. Her bed was against the west wall, and sometimes at night she would press her hand flat against the gyprock, feeling its cool, paint-pimpled skin, and through its terranean dampness, wick herself — for it went beyond imagining — back to Kits Beach, and Monika. "Are you busking?" Monika would ask, and to Sabie's *no,* would calmly add, "Well, one day, then." And then, through Sabie's hand, the two of them would squiggle their backs into the clammy sand and stare into the starless sky until sleep came.

There were none of Monika's probing, heart-turning, bone-touching questions, not from Monika, not from Colin, Margaux or Dylan. Sabie missed that most of all.

"Hi, Sabe," Colin called, once he'd reached their little rest site. She caught her breath; that was Parker's nickname for her. Or had Parker learned it from Colin all those years ago? She strained to see if the answer was in his face, but there was nothing there but the joy of the moment. Colin stood smiling down at her with his gentle, round face, one hand tousling Margaux's hair affectionately. "Ready for lunch?"

"Okay."

Sabie wiggled her feet into their thick, warm

socks and slipped into her slide-on sneakers. Then, slowly, she walked up the sparsely-grassed embankment, wondering at how cracked and thirsty the bald ground looked, even after the recent thaw. Only when she approached the crest of the hill, near the waiting trio, did she lift her head again to look at them and beyond them, to the open, rolling, stubbly distance.

Being in Vancouver, surrounded by mountains, thought Sabie, was a lot like being held in the palm of someone's hand. God's hand, if you believed in God the way Estelle had. But here, you were surrounded by forever. The rolling land went on endlessly, no matter how far you ran into it.

"Did you guys ever think that this place is like one of those never-ending linen towel-roller things they have in bathrooms sometimes?" Sabie asked, accepting a Spartan apple from Colin and biting into it. "You know, the kind where you pull clean towel out the front and dirty towel goes in the back." She remembered her habit of talking around food and she stowed the apple chunk politely in her cheek.

"Huh?" Colin swooped Dylan up onto his shoulders and looked out at the horizon as if he really might see a towel roller.

"Did you ever think that maybe life is like that, too, an endless loop?"

"I don't think those towel dispensers are really loops," said Colin. "I think they're —"

"Life's like a loop of what?" Margaux asked. She held out a seed-topped bun to Colin.

Sabie considered. She felt full of something she

wanted to tell them, but couldn't say what. "A loop of everything, all the stuff that has gone before, and all the new stuff, woven together; like that? And to get to the future, you've got to grab onto the whole bit and pull. You can't just chop off the past and leave it hanging there. "

"Um . . . " Margaux glanced at Colin and then smiled warmly at Sabie, showing the crooked tooth that she usually took care to hide.

"Like a fan belt?" suggested Colin, who liked to fix cars. "A fan belt is a loop."

Sabie laughed. "Never mind," she said. They never got what she was talking about. But that was okay. Life was about lots of things besides the meaning of life. It was about how spaghetti feels in your hand before you drop it into the pot, about Dylan growing into the next size up of diapers, about playing Risk with Colin and Margaux and nobody wishing for one second to be anyplace else. And about reaching out to a bunch of ordinary people who want to love you and saying yes, this will be my family.

Monika had been right. Life is a kind of dance. Estelle had been right, too. It is a struggle. Sabie knew there were all kinds of questions out there that she had yet to ask, and that asking them was going to take her whole life. She didn't know yet whether there would be a Morty in her life, or a Candace, or someone who could be even the teeniest bit like Monika.

But for now, standing with her new family in the hot, stubble-parting wind, Sabie knew that she wasn't just going to run with whatever life threw her, as Monika had shown her on the beach. What Sabie really planned to do was to reach out and, as much as possible, grab what was good.